I0538864

The Ghost
of
Sherlock Holmes

By

Paul Voodini

First edition published in 2016
© Copyright 2016
Paul Voodini

The right of Paul Voodini to be identified as the author of this work has been asserted by him in accordance with the Copyright, Designs and Patents Act 1998.

All rights reserved. No reproduction, copy or transmission of this publication may be made without express prior written permission. No paragraph of this publication may be reproduced, copied or transmitted except with express prior written permission or in accordance with the provisions of the Copyright Act 1956 (as amended). Any person who commits any unauthorised act in relation to this publication may be liable to criminal prosecution and civil claims for damage.

Although every effort has been made to ensure the accuracy of the information contained in this book, as of the date of publication, nothing herein should be construed as giving advice. The opinions expressed herein are those of the author and not of MX Publishing.

Paperback ISBN 978-1-78092-983-5
ePub ISBN 978-1-78092-984-2
PDF ISBN 978-1-78092-985-9

Published in the UK by MX Publishing
335 Princess Park Manor, Royal Drive, London, N11 3GX
www.mxpublishing.co.uk
Cover design by Brian Belanger

The Ghost of Sherlock Holmes

*

A Sherlock Holmes Inspired Yarn, Accompanied by a Compendium of Mind-Reading & Magic Presentations, Utilising Playing Cards, Pendulums, and Other Such Common Objects.

By

Mr. Paul Voodini

Contents

Credits

Dedicated to all the authors, script writers, actors, directors, and other creative-types who have kept the creative flame of Sherlock Holmes alive and well for the last century and a half.

*

Many thanks to my wonderful children, Lucy and James, who prove to me each and every day that magic is real.

This book would not have been possible were it not for the generosity and belief of the following people, whose support meant that The Ghost of Sherlock Holmes could be given the spark of life. To each and every one of this book's producers, thank you.

Alan Penman

Tim Gaffney

Jimmy Ledbetter

Max McLaughlin

Jeremy B. Holstein

Robert R. Schake

Faith Saffron Ejankowski

Kathy Caulfield

Pauline Brown

Louis Loriot

Mr. Darkness

Kris De Ruysscher

Michael Henry, PhD

Russell J. Hall

Paul Noffsinger

Thank you!

New Year's Eve,
1922

1922

"These are the things that we have seen..."

1922 begins with the British Empire at the zenith of its size and influence, covering a quarter of the globe and with King George 5th ruling over one in four of the earth's inhabitants.

1st January – Transport & General Workers' Union formed.

7th January – the Anglo-Irish Treaty is ratified in Eire.

12th January – British government releases last of Irish prisoners captured during the War of Independence.

By the end of January, an influenza outbreak would claim over 800 victims.

29th April – Huddersfield Town beat Preston North End 1 – 0 to win the FA Cup, held at Stamford Bridge in London.

1st June – official formation of the Royal Ulster Constabulary.

22nd June – Irish Republican Army agents assassinate Field Marshall Sir Henry Wilson. The perpetrators are apprehended and sentenced to death on 18th July.

18th October – the British Broadcasting Company (BBC) is formed.

4th November – British archaeologist Howard Carter discovers entrance to tomb of Tutankhamen in Egypt's Valley of the Kings.

14th November – the BBC begins radio broadcasts from London.

15th November – the Conservative party wins the General Election. The Labour party becomes the UK's second largest party, over-taking the Liberals.

7th December – the Parliament of Northern Ireland votes to remain part of the UK.

1923

"These are the things that are yet to be..."

16th February – archaeologist Howard Carter and his team opens the burial chamber of Tutankhamen.

26th April – wedding of Prince Albert, Duke of York (later George 6th) and Lady Elizabeth Bowes-Lyon (Queen Elizabeth the Queen Mother) takes place in Westminster Abbey, London.

28th April – the Empire Stadium, Wembley is opened to the public for the first time and hosts the FA Cup between Bolton Wanderers and West Ham United. Mounted police (including one famously white horse) clear crowds from the pitch.

23rd May – Stanley Baldwin becomes Prime Minister following Bonar Law's resignation due to ill health.

31st July – the Liquor Act makes it illegal to sell alcohol to the under-18s.

28th September – the Radio Times is first published, detailing radio programmes to be broadcast by the BBC.

6th December – the Conservative Party, led by Stanley Baldwin, wins the General Election, but without enough seats to hold a majority.

31st December – the BBC broadcasts the chimes of Big Ben for the first time.

Also in this year, *Littlewoods Pools* is formed by Liverpool businessman John Moores.

Elsewhere in the world, political scientist Henry Kissenger is born, and German physicist Wilhelm Rontgen, discoverer of X-rays, dies.

Your attendance is cordially requested at a New Year's Eve dinner party on Sunday, 31st December, 1922 at the Host's London residence, whereby a four course meal will be served and amusement provided by a demonstration of the Host's collection of Sherlock Holmes artefacts and antiques.

Aperitifs to be served at 7 o'clock *post meridian.*

Our Cast

The Host – the mysterious host of this evening's dinner party is an enigmatic character. Who is he and what are his motivations?

Mr. Campbell – a criminal lawyer and long-time acquaintance of the host, does Campbell know the host through his professional life? And if so, in what capacity would our host have needed the services of a criminal lawyer?

Mr. Jones – an undertaker by trade, Mr. Jones is the very embodiment of the *sombre* stereotype of his trade, although it has been noted that his penchant for brandy and whisky means that he could never be described as *sober*.

Dr. Kris De Ruysscher – a world renowned phrenologist from Belgium, Dr. De Ruysscher is in London to lecture to the Royal Society. But why has he been invited to the host's dinner party, and what, exactly, is it that a phrenologist *does*?

Mrs. Carriger – the wife of a good friend of the host, Mrs. Carriger's officer husband tasked the host to take care of his wife and daughter while he was away serving with the British Army in Jordan, helping to put down the Kura Rebellion.

Miss Carriger – the daughter of Mrs. Carriger, Miss Carriger finds herself in the unenviable position of being in her early 20s, unmarried, and without even a *beau* to speak of! Her mother is worried that her daughter may end up a spinster, although Miss Carriger herself seems entirely nonplussed by her precarious position.

Mrs. Hudson – a widow and family friend of the host, she enjoys the company of others but finds that, in these twilight years, she tires easily.

NEW YEAR'S EVE, 1922...

"I am a collector of... *oddities*," I smiled as I sat before the log fire, observing the small band of friends and acquaintances who had accepted my invite to spend New Year's Eve as my guests at a most unusual dinner party, the ladies gracing us with their best evening gowns and the gentlemen resplendent in black tie.

The date was December 31st, 1922. After surviving the horrors of the Great War, little did we know of the horrors that still awaited us as the 20th Century wore on – the Great Depression, another World War, countless dead in the cause of freedom, and the breakdown of Empire as the baton of world-leader was handed to our American cousins across the Atlantic. But that was all for the future. For the here and now, the year 1922 still had a few hours left in it and I intended to employ them profitably.

On a small table to my left lay an intriguing collection; several decks of playing cards, a single pendulum, and two silver finger rings. The silver rings caught the light from the roaring log fire and twinkled most beguilingly. Once I was sure my guests were seated comfortably and my butler George had furnished them with a tipple to chase away the late December chills, I began my narrative...

"We have all heard, I take it, of the great detective Sherlock Holmes? That celebrated denizen of the Strand magazine?" I asked.

There were murmurs of agreement from my guests. I would have been most perturbed if any of my guests had not heard of the Master of Deduction, who, at the time, was perhaps the owner of the most recognisable name in the English speaking world.

"Fictional character isn't he?" asked the bruff undertaker Jones, as he helped himself to another generous snifter of brandy. It appeared that to Jones, a decanted bottle was not so much a luxury to be savoured as a challenge to be mastered.

"A fictional character? Well, so we are assured," I acquiesced, "but were you aware that many of his exploits were in fact based on truths? Did you know that Arthur Conan Doyle actually based the character of Holmes on his old medical school lecturer, Dr. Joseph Bell? A man so observant and skilled in his craft that he could diagnose illnesses and describe in perfect detail the life history of a patient purely on sight, without the need for discussion?"

The room looked on in silence. I appeared to have captured the attention of my guests. I smiled inwardly.

"I have, over the past few years," I continued, "become quietly fascinated with both the fictional Sherlock Holmes character and also the truths and facts that lie behind his

16

exploits. These meagre few objects," I pointed at the packs of playing cards, the pendulum, and the finger rings, "are, you could say, souvenirs of this fascination. Each one is, in some way or other, associated with the Great Detective or his creator, Arthur Conan Doyle."

"I say," interrupted Campbell, the lawyer, leaning forward in his chair and looking around himself, as if searching for something, "are we to be fed tonight? Only my stomach is rumbling something awful!" He laughed mirthlessly and eyed his fellow guests for support.

"All in good time, my dear Campbell," I smiled. "Food will of course be served. But first I'd like to demonstrate, if I may, one of the peculiarities of my collection."

I leant to my left and took a packet of playing cards from the table.

"One of the skills that Dr. Bell was able to astonish his students with was his ability to instantly memorise any number of objects, words, or images. I believe that the phrase 'photographic memory' is starting to be used to describe such extraordinary feats of memory.

"To demonstrate this ability, Dr. Bell would use a packet of playing cards. Indeed, he would use *this very* packet of playing cards, acquired from a somewhat dishonest cleaner-woman at Edinburgh University whose duties, besides purloining items that caught her eye, included the cleaning of Dr. Bell's quarters. Once the cleaner's 'light fingered' exploits were discovered, she was dismissed on the spot but managed to escape from the university compound before the police could arrive to apprehend her.

"Several months later it came to my attention that this female magpie had in her possession a packet of cards stolen from Dr. Bell himself. I knew I had to have them and so I set off on something of an adventure to Edinburgh, travelling aboard the famous Flying Scotsman train, to locate the thieving cleaner and her ill-gotten possessions.

"I have several contacts in Scotland Yard, I shan't bore you with the sordid details of the whys and the hows, but suffice to say that several little birds here in London had words with several little birds on the Edinburgh police force, and before too long I had a name and an address, and I was on my way!"

"All sounds very cloak and dagger," said Campbell, the lawyer, as he knocked his pipe out into a crystal ashtray.

"Oh I assure you, sir, that the truth is far more ordinary and mundane. A few telephone calls, a few favours returned, that is all," I smiled. Campbell huffed into his pipe as though he did not think it sounded very ordinary and mundane at all. I paid him no heed and continued.

"The journey from King's Cross station in London to Waverley station in Edinburgh took a little over eight hours which gave me plenty of time to relax, to read, to eat, and even to get my hair cut at the newly opened barbershop aboard the train!"

"A barbershop aboard a train!" gasped the delightful Miss Carriger, bedecked as she was in a shimmering emerald ball gown, cut in accordance with the latest fashions. "What an age of wonders we live in, truly! And how was Edinburgh? I would dearly love to visit one day."

"Edinburgh is a fine city," I said, "and much deserving of the title 'Empire's Second City'. But, much like our own beloved London, it has its darker corners, its rookeries and rat-runs, and it was in one such rookery that I located the thieving cleaner and the stolen deck of playing cards. The cleaner-woman was naturally very suspicious of me at first, she wondered if I might not be what people of her class call a 'copper'. But I reassured her, and when I pressed a few coins into her palm, she soon relaxed and invited me into her modest home.

"When I describe the woman's home as being 'modest', I am of course being polite. Not wanting to upset any of you with the gory details, I will simply say that the place was small, smelt terribly of boiled cabbage, and seated in one corner was the woman's surly husband, who eyed me menacingly as though deciding whether or not there was any profit in murdering me on the spot."

"Oh my!" gasped Mrs. Hudson, putting a frail hand to her mouth.

"Gosh!" exclaimed Miss Carriger. "How terribly exciting!"

Miss Carriger's mother *tut-tutted* her daughter and said, "There is nothing remotely exciting about the lower classes, my dear."

I held up my hands to apologise for causing the ladies such disquiet, and continued, "Suffice to say that money was exchanged, Dr. Bell's playing cards were handed over, and I beat a hasty retreat from the hovels of Edinburgh. And now, here I am today, brandishing those very same playing cards and ready to demonstrate for you the very same mental feat that Dr. Bell would utilise to impress and astound his students. That is," I paused, "if you would like me to?"

There were general murmurs of agreement, and Miss Carriger, under the ever-observant gaze of her mother, nodded her head enthusiastically.

"Very well," I said, "then I shall proceed. Please keep in mind the fact that failure is a likely outcome here. What I am about to attempt stretches to breaking point the cognitive abilities of the human brain. But never-the-less, let us try."

Dr. BELL'S PARTY PIECE

I took the playing cards from their box and gave them a shuffle. I then handed the cards to Miss Carriger's mother and invited her to also mix them up. She protested that she hardly knew how to handle playing cards, much less shuffle them, but then her dexterous display with the cards made a lie of her protests and indicated to me, at least, that she enjoyed many an afternoon at the gin rummy table.

Once the assembled company were happy that the cards were truly mixed and nobody could possibly know the order of the cards, I held the pack before my eyes (faces towards me) and riffled through them. As the 52 cards flashed before my eyes, I attempted to memorise their order at lightning speed. I looked studiously into the middle distance and then repeated the process, once more attempting to memorise the order of the playing cards.

"This is very difficult," I explained. "I'm attempting to memorise the order of the cards, and it's a skill that is rather hard to develop. I fear I am still learning the skills required. I am a poor match for Dr. Bell, who by all accounts was rather good at this kind of thing. Hopefully you will not hold it against me if I take one more quick flick through the cards?"

Once again I held the cards up before my face and quickly riffled through them, allowing each card to come momentarily into sight. I then held the cards in a ribbon spread between my two hands and offered them to Mrs. Carriger.

"Please," I said, "take one card, keep it face down, look at it but don't let me see it. Please do this is as quickly as you can. My memory of the deck's order is gossamer thin and could evaporate at any moment."

The lady selected one card, and pulled it face down from the ribbon spread pack.

"Please keep the card safe," I instructed her. "And please, can I ask for silence. My memory of the deck is fading fast and I fear that any distraction will scatter it finally to the four winds."

Once again I held the deck up before my face. "I shall now attempt to discern which card is missing from the order. If my memory of the deck of cards can just hold true, perhaps I can spot the missing card. But perhaps not. Let us see."

Again I held the deck before my face and riffled through them, trying - almost in vain - to spot a hole in my memory where a card should have been. Was it possible to memorise a whole deck in a few short seconds and then deduce which single card had been removed from that deck? Surely not, but I had promised that I would try and so try I would.

I placed the cards back down onto the top of the table and closed my eyes. Under my breath I muttered the names of cards and their order as best as I could remember them. Eventually I opened my eyes. The room was hushed, and expectation prickled in the air like Mr. Edison's electricity.

I was unsure of myself, but finally I muttered, "The Seven of Spades? The Seven... of Spades?"

Mrs. Carriger gasped and held a gloved hand to her mouth. Then she breathed, "Yes!" and turned over her selected card. It was indeed the seven of Spades. The guests broke into a spontaneous round of applause.

"I say!" bellowed Campbell, the lawyer. "Jolly good show, old man!"

"Now," I smiled, "who's for a spot of dinner? I think I may have earned it!"

*

Our Host's Secret

I suppose, dear reader, that you will be interested to know how I managed to accomplish this incredible feat of memory? Well, allow me to enlighten you. The secret is, in fact, childishly simple. The deck of cards I was using was marked. I know, how awful of me! All that talk of developing memory skills was pure bunkum – what a rotter I am, and no mistake!

For those of you who are not fluent in the errant ways of the magician, let me explain about marked decks. A marked deck is a deck of cards that has some image, picture, number, or *mark* on the back each and every card that allows the user to know what the value of the card is on the front of the card. So for example, a card may be marked with a small JS. In this example, such a mark would indicate that the card was the Jack of Spades. JS = Jack of Spades. This is just a simple example, and methods of marking a deck of cards range from the childishly simple to the extraordinarily intricate.

Historically magicians have marked their own decks of cards using their own systems, but as the 20th Century advanced into the 21st Century, so factory-made marked cards have become readily available if you know where to look for them.

Now you are probably wondering how a man such a myself, who is living in the year 1922, can be aware of 20th and 21st Century developments? The answer to that sticky question is that I do, in fact, own a time machine and have, on occasion, travelled the corridors of time and space. But, alas, that is another story for another publication, and you will, I hope, forgive me if I do not go into details at this juncture. Instead, let us return to the matter at hand...

If you wish to locate a marked deck of cards for your own nefarious uses, may I suggest using what is known as the *internet*. Firstly, use a search engine to discover an on-line magic shop (there are, you may be surprised to discover, hundreds of them to be found). Then use the website's search function to look for marked cards.

A word of warning – styles of marking decks of cards do vary wildly, and it may take a little research and experimentation to discover which style of marking works best for you.

Magicians (and gamblers with dubious morals) have been using marked cards for several centuries. Marked cards work well because the marks themselves are all-but invisible to the untrained eye. If you do not know the marking system being used, there is every chance that you will never spot the mark no matter how long you examine the back of the card.

So now that you are aware of my little secret, how does one employ this knowledge to appear to be a master of memory? Let me explain further...

While the volunteer you are using (on this occasion the volunteer was Mrs Carriger) selects a card from the ribbon spread deck, the performer spots the mark of the card being selected. It is as straightforward as that. As Mrs Carriger was taking one card from the deck being offered to her, I spied the mark on the back of said card. All the rest is window-dressing and play-acting. BUT – do not dismiss the power of this demonstration! Your audience will genuinely believe that you have some manner of enhanced memory power and they will be in awe of you.

Well, maybe they won't really be in awe of you. They won't be in awe of you if you mumble your words, giggle nervously, or, worst of all, reveal the secret afterwards either out of guilt because you've been 'lying' or in an attempt to appear 'clever' in front of family and friends. If you really want them to be in awe of you, do not dismiss the necessity to put on a good show. When riffling through the deck, actually attempt to memorise as much of the deck as you possibly can. Why not? You may as well attempt to actually do this for real! Have a bit of fun with it! If you actually attempt to memorise the deck (you won't get very far, trust me, but give it a go), it will make selling your performance to your audience so much easier. They will see the concentration on your face, they will notice the mental effort you are exerting, and they will instinctively pick up on the fact that you are doing this for real.

Play the role (look up 'method acting') and you will sell the routine. Any notion of outright trickery will be dismissed by the audience. They may believe that there is a *method* involved, but they will not view that method as trickery. If your audience demand repeat demonstrations in an attempt to catch you out, simply explain that the strain upon your mind is too much, and that your talent fades as you become tired. This explanation makes you appear even more mysterious and wondrous!

When the card is being selected by your volunteer, you can always control how quickly that card is pulled from the deck (in case it takes you a moment or two for you to spot the mark). By exerting different amounts of pressure on the cards with your fingers, you can control how difficult or easy it is to pull the card out, giving you an extra precious second should you need it. *Et viola*! You are perceived of as a *bone fide* memory master!

*

Sherlock Holmes Says...

Hold on there, dear chap! While I appreciate the simplicity of your marked deck of cards, I feel duty bound to explain that it is entirely possible, with a little training, to achieve this memory feat quite genuinely. The skill that needs to be used is known as a *Memory Palace*. Allow me to explain.

A memory palace is an imaginary building that exists only in your mind and in which are placed things that you may want to remember. Because the items you are wanting to remember are placed within an imaginary building, it makes the items easier to remember and easier to recall. After playing around and experimenting with various memory palaces, I now find that it is almost impossible to actually forget items placed within until I actually make the conscious decision to let go of them!

If the idea of a memory palace is new to you, I would like you to carry out a little experiment, just to prove to you the power of the principle. However, I will first explain to you exactly what my *personal* memory palace is, and then I will ask you to create your own memory palace in your mind.

My memory palace is not a palace at all; it is in fact the memory of the house that I occupied at 221b Baker Street, and in which I engaged many a happy hour discussing death, murder, and the criminal classes with my good friend Dr John Watson. Although the memories attached to 221b Baker Street occurred close to 20 years ago, the emotions and happiness attached to this location are still strong enough to make it a very potent memory palace for me. I find that the more personal the memory palace, the more powerful it will prove to be.

The tour of my memory palace begins at the front door. This is location #1 and I imagine myself ringing on the doorbell as I was often forced to do, having once again misplaced my damnable keys. The door then opens and I imagine my dear Mrs Hudson smiling and greeting me. This is location #2. I then walk into the living room.

Watson is sitting there smoking a pipe. This is location #3. Next I imagine myself walking into the dining room. I remember us partaking of Christmas dinner in there, and this is location #4.

Next I walk into the kitchen and remember Mrs Hudson concocting some more delightful meals for us. This is location #5. Then I wander out into the back garden where I would enjoy tending my bees on summer afternoons. This is location #6.

From there it is back into the house and I walk up the stairs. This is location #7. I walk into my bedroom where, unable to sleep, I would often play my violin, and this is location #8. Then it is into Mrs Hudson's bedroom, a dark and mysterious place that I rarely saw the inside of, and the memory of which still sends chills down my spine! This is location #9.

From there into the bedroom often used by Watson, location #10, the bathroom is location #11, and then up into the dusty old attic which is location #12.

In this very simplified description of my memory palace there are 12 separate locations in which memories can be placed. I can, and often do, expand upon this memory palace, adding other locations such as the shops along Baker Street and the small front garden. But for a simple demonstration, 12 locations shall suffice.

Now let us experiment with remembering a simple shopping list using my memory palace. I do not expect you to try and do this yourself yet, after all my memory palace means absolutely nothing to you, but by reading an explanation as to how I employ my memory palace, when it comes to your turn to do this with your own memory palace, you will understand exactly what is being asked of you.

The shopping list: bacon, tomatoes, milk, sausages, cheese, tea, wine, and soap. Now, normally, without the use of my memory palace, I would be unable to remember this short list without writing it down. Invariably I would leave the shop without at least one item, much to the chagrin of Mrs. Hudson who would chastise me for being such a *Forgetful Horace*. However, this is how the memory palace helps me to remember such a list, and in fact makes it all but impossible for me to forget any item:

I imagine myself ringing on the doorbell of 221b. It is early in the morning and I am carrying **bacon** for breakfast. The door opens and Mrs Hudson smiles and welcomes me. However, she is carrying a large paper bag full of **tomatoes**, and she remarks that the tomatoes will go well with the bacon for breakfast. We walk into the dining room where Watson is seated. He is drinking from a bottle of **milk**, and some of the milk is spilling out of the side of his mouth and is dripping onto his shirt. From there we go into the dining room. I remember having Christmas dinner in this room one memorable year, but on this occasion, rather than the traditional goose, we are being served with **sausages**.

I then enter the kitchen. I remember Mrs Hudson making cauliflower cheese, and I hand her a block of **cheese** to grate over the vegetables. We walk into the garden. It is a nice sunny day and I am enjoying an invigorating cup of **tea**.

Next I am walking up the stairs, heading towards my bedroom while carrying a large glass of **wine** in the hope that this alcoholic beverage will aid me to sleep. Sadly, I cannot sleep, so I walk into Watson's bedroom to regale him with a rendition on my violin. Watson looks up at me as I enter, but he is washing his face in a bowl and has **soap** covering his visage. This concludes the tour and I have successfully remembered each item.

When I have finished shopping, the items simply slip from my memory palace and are no longer stored in my memory palace. This can be achieved consciously by thinking to myself, "I no longer need to remember these items, they are erased from my memory palace", but I find that this is not necessary. The erasure of the items seems to occur naturally by itself, on a subconscious level.

Now, dear reader, what I would like you to do is create your very own memory palace. As I stated earlier, this always works better when you use a building that you know, can remember in great detail, and that, perhaps most importantly, you have some emotional attachment to.

Perhaps you would like to choose a home you remember well, or the home of a partner, friend, or someone you are very fond of? An old school that holds a lot of happy memories? Anywhere at all will fit the bill, as long as you feel some kind of emotional bond with it.

The important aspect of your memory palace is that it has rooms and/or locations contained within it, and that within these rooms you can 'store' pieces of information that you need to remember. In my own example, the house had many rooms, the living room, dining room, kitchen, bedrooms, etc. The more locations/rooms that a memory palace has, the better.

In the first instance, it would be good if you could close your eyes, imagine the building, imagine yourself walking around it, and see if you can find twelve individual locations in which items that need to be remembered (such as items on a shopping list) can be placed.

In my example, I always imagine that Watson and Mrs Hudson are there with me and often I will imagine them walking around the memory palace with me. This helps to reinforce the memory and reinforce the items that need to be remembered. It gives the memorised list a human aspect that my mind can latch on to, and also gives me the opportunity to give the items to be remembered a slightly humorous angle which also helps. For instance, in the example with the shopping list Mrs Hudson was carrying a huge bag of tomatoes, Watson was drinking milk but it was spilling out of the sides of the glass, the Christmas dinner was sausages, etc. Adding a human angle and making the memory slightly surreal reinforces the items to be remembered.

If by now you have settled on a memory palace of your own, discover what people are there with you. Perhaps friends and family who used to live or visit the place that you have chosen. Decide what rooms these people will reside in, and perhaps chose one person to accompany you. Someone who you have fond memories of and who you would like to accompany you every time you visit your own memory palace. Someone who will, perhaps, open the door, smile at you, and welcome you in on each visit.

There now follows a list of 12 items. I want you to imagine yourself entering your memory palace and placing each of these items in a separate location within the memory palace. Remember to add a touch of the bizarre to proceedings; for example, within the list is a ladder. Imagine the ladder in a certain location, and imagine a person (friend, family member) at the top of the ladder, asking for your help to get down. They have found themselves trapped, but it is still quite a humorous situation. Add the human angle, add something slightly surreal, and that item will be fixed firmly in your memory palace for as long as you want it to be.

Hat.

Banana.

Bunch of flowers.

Notepad.

Telephone.

Ladder.

Candles.

A collection of books.

Cup of coffee.

Newspaper.

Photo-frame.

A large typewriter.

Do not expect miracles the first time you do this. If you fail to remember all the items (and I imagine that if this is the first time you have tried this you will probably get stuck on one item, perhaps two), you may not have added enough of the human angle and enough of the surreal/humorous aspect. Once you get used to applying those aspects, it becomes very simple. The 'trick', and one balks at describing it thus, when remembering a list is to add the human and the bizarre, and to really *see* in your mind's eye these events taking place.

Although utilising a memory palace and imagining oneself walking through it, placing objects to be remembered into each room, may seem a somewhat complex memory to conjure up, the fact is that the walk through of the memory palace should really only take seconds to create. You will find, with only a little practice, that you will also be able to create these memories in mere seconds yourself. For example, when going to the shops, I remember my list in my head as I put on my hat, coat, and scarf. It is that quick.

If you struggled with remembering all the items the first time around, please go back and try again. Notice this time how much easier it is, and how much more successful you are. And you will also notice how, once it is appropriate, you can forget all the items, wipe the slate clean, and your memory palace is empty and ready for use again.

So now we have an almost fool-proof technique for remembering 12 items. What happens if we want to remember more than 12 items? Simple. We expand upon the original memory palace.

The memory palace you have created in your mind is the 'basic' model, the 'classic' version. This is the place that you will generally use, 12 rooms or locations usually being enough for most day-to-day applications of the technique. However, if you are using the technique for larger demonstrations, you will need to remember more items. In order to do this, what you need to do is add more locations. My personal method is to imagine myself walking home around the streets that surround 221b Baker Street. This walk (and it is a walk that I undertook many, many times) gives me many new locations. You can perhaps do the same with your memory palace, or add a bus/taxi ride, or even imagine yourself walking around the grounds of the building. If there are floors or rooms left unexplored in the original memory palace, utilise these. Once you have 12 locations under your belt, it is a relatively simple matter to introduce 'add-on' locations.

If, after exhausting my walk around 221b's locale, I still need more locations in which to deposit items to be remembered, I imagine myself re-arriving at the front door of 221b and I take a 'second lap'. This is relatively easy to do with a little practice, the mind is very clever at being able to differentiate between the first tour around the full memory palace and the second tour. This will take a little practice though, but once done will open up the possibility of up to 52 items.

52 items? Hmm. What could possibly take up 52 locations? Ah, yes! A freely shuffled deck of playing cards, a notion introduced to us by our dubious host!

Using the memory palace technique previously discussed, it is possible to memorise, within a minute or two, a freely shuffled deck of 52 cards. But there is a problem. The memory palace system works best when you are able to, as we have seen, inject a human angle and a touch of the surreal. For example, Watson with milk spilling from his mouth. This is easy enough for the royal cards in a regular deck of cards; perhaps we can imagine the Queen of Hearts screaming "Off with their heads!" or the Jack of Hearts stealing the tarts. But what about the numbers? The numbers, for example the 8 of Clubs, have no human qualities, and it is difficult to inject any sense of humour into proceedings to help remember the card in the correct location. How then do we do this?

In order to make the numbers easier to remember, and add an element to help us 'humanise' them, we use a number/rhyming system. For the numbers 1 – 10, these are the rhymes. I shall explain how to use them in a moment.

1 – in our instance, with playing cards in mind, the 1 is the Ace. This is relatively simple to remember as a great big representation of the appropriate suit; perhaps a giant diamond for the Ace of Diamonds. I shall expand on this shortly.

2 – rhymes with shoe. 2 is a shoe.

3 – rhymes with tree. 3 is a tree.

4 – rhymes with door. 4 is a door.

5 – rhymes with hive. 5 is a hive.

6 – is similar to sex. 6 is sex (*ahem*, apologies to any ladies who may be present).

7 – rhymes with heaven. 7 is heaven.

8 – rhymes with mate. 8 is mate.

9 – rhymes with sign. 9 is mine.

10 – rhymes with men. 10 is men.

Therefore, in order to remember playing cards, we visualise them thus:

Ace of Diamonds – a great big, giant diamond.

2 of Diamonds – a golden shoe encrusted with diamonds.

3 of Diamonds – a marvellous tree that has diamonds for fruit hanging from it.

4 of Diamonds – a sparkly door encrusted with diamonds.

5 of Diamonds – a sparkly bee hive with diamonds instead of bees flying in and out of it.

6 of Diamonds – having sex with the man or lady of your dreams, surrounded by bowls full of diamonds.

7 of Diamonds – the gates to heaven encrusted with diamonds.

8 of Diamonds – your good friend (in working class parlance, your *mate*) offering you a bowl full of diamonds as a gift.

9 of Diamonds – a diamond that belongs to you. You pick it up very jealously, put it into your pocket and tell everyone that "It' mine!"

10 of Diamonds – a gang of men (diamond miners?) arguing over who owns a diamond. The diamond keeps slipping out of their hands as they fight, and flies across the room.

Jack of Diamonds – a very flash young man, very confident, covered in jewellery and diamonds.

Queen of Diamonds – a woman with too much make-up on, dripping with gold and diamonds, and wearing very pink vibrant clothes.

King of Diamonds – an old man wearing a crown and inappropriate diamond jewellery. Big rings on his fingers, encrusted with diamonds.

Ace of Hearts – a giant heart, pumping away by itself, blood pouring from it (remember, make it surreal!).

2 of Hearts – a red shoe with a heart in it, blood seeping out of the seams.

3 of Hearts – a tree with hearts for fruit, blood dripping from the branches.

4 of Hearts – a bright red door with a window in it, looking through the window you see an operation theatre where open-heart surgery is taking place.

5 of Hearts – a red hive with blood seeping from its pores. Perhaps small hearts buzzing around instead of bees.

6 of Hearts – having sex with the man or lady of your dreams and being worried you were about to have a heart attack!

7 of Hearts – people in heaven, sobbing because they died from a broken heart.

8 of Hearts – a friend (a *mate*) telling you that he had a heart attack, he is clutching his chest.

9 of Hearts – your heart. You pick it up very jealously and scream, "It's mine!"

10 of Hearts – a group of men who meet each week to discuss how they survived a fatal heart condition; a kind of heart related support group.

Jack of Hearts – a typical knave running away with the queen's tarts.

Queen of Hearts – the queen screaming 'off with their heads!'

King of Hearts – the queen's husband, trying to placate her and offering her his heart instead of the tarts.

Ace of Spades – in my mind I always equate spades with the tarot suit, the swords. In Italian, a sword is *spada*, and so the origin of the word 'spade' is the Italian for sword. This makes it easier to remember. Sword = spade. A giant sword stuck in a rock, a little like in the Arthurian legend.

2 of Spades – a shoe with a dangerous looking dagger (sword) sticking out of the toe.

3 of Spades – a tree with tiny swords hanging from the branches. A warning sign near-by telling people to beware of falling swords.

4 of Spades – a door with a dagger (sword) for a handle. Having to be careful to open it.

5 of Spades – a beehive with tiny swords buzzing around. Being stung by one of the swords, which gives you a little cut.

6 of Spades – having sex with the man or lady of your dreams. He/she is a prince/princess and you are a brave knight (!), having to be careful where your sword goes while you have sex.

7 of Spades – Heaven is guarded by knights with giant swords, ready to propel an attack by the devil.

8 of Spades – a friends (a *mate*) trying to pick up a giant sword. It is far too big and heavy for him, and the scene is quite comical.

9 of Spades – the sword in this room is yours. You pick it up and tell everyone that "It is mine!"

10 of Spades – men fighting each other with their giant swords!

Jack of Spades – Jack the Ripper with a very sharp knife (sword) creeping through an alleyway.

Queen of Spades – Joan of Arc, in armour brandishing a sword.

King of Spades – King Henry 6th in armour and carrying sword, about to fight Joan of Arc.

Ace of Clubs – a giant club, like that carried by a caveman, on display in a museum.

2 of Clubs – a caveman wearing some very fashionable shoes. He is finding it difficult to stand in them and is using a club as a support.

3 of Clubs – a tree with tiny clubs hanging from the branches, a caveman asleep underneath it, holding a big club in his hands.

4 of Clubs – the door is locked so you have to use a giant club to break it down.

5 of Clubs – a caveman hitting a beehive with a club, and then having to flee from the pursuing bees!

6 of Clubs – a caveman hitting a woman over the head with a club in order to...well, you know. I shall not go into detail for fear of upsetting those of a nervous disposition.

7 of Clubs – heaven is full of cavemen, all holding clubs.

8 of Clubs – your friend (your *mate*) is a caveman, perhaps for a fancy dress party, and is proudly showing you his club.

9 of Clubs – fighting with a caveman because he has stolen your club. "It's mine!" you shout.

10 of Clubs – cavemen gathered together, there are no women, this is a men-only club and a sign at the door points this out.

Jack of Clubs – Jack the Ripper has lost his knife and is having to make-do with a club. He isn't happy about it, and hides it behind his back in an embarrassed kind of way.

Queen of Clubs – a female cavewoman, shouting at the cavemen and waving her club above her head.

King of Clubs – a caveman wearing a golden crown. The crown is far too big for him and he has to keep pushing it back on to his head with his club.

Of course you do not need to use my own personal memory aids as listed above. By all means create your own – ones that would be more personal to you and which you think you would be able to remember more readily than the ones that I have provided.

With these visualisation tools/ideas in place, it is then a relatively simple task to place them into rooms/areas of your memory palace as required, and for them to be recalled on demand by imagining yourself walking around your memory palace and recounting what you see there. In this way are you able to memorise an entire deck of cards within a matter of minutes.

Have a go now, and see how well you do. The first two or three attempts are likely to come to an end around the '12 cards correctly recounted' mark. Soon after you should be able to recount 18 or 20, and then 25. By practising for a few days, you will be able to remember more and more until you reach your goal of memorising an entire, freely shuffled deck.

To practice by yourself, simply take a deck of cards, shuffle them fairly, then turn over each card in turn, memorise them by placing them into your memory palace, one card per room/location, until you have completed the entire deck. Obviously retain the original sequence of cards, then recount each card, one at a time, turning over the appropriate card after you have stated which you believe it is, and see how many you get right.

As a performance piece for friends and family, it is not necessary to demonstrate the memorisation of an entire deck. You can cut off half the deck, and simply use this smaller packet for the demonstration. Alternatively use the entire deck but only memorise around half. Then once you have recounted all of the cards that you have memorised, simply push the rest of the cards to one side and say, "And that's enough of that! I think I have made my point!" the implication being, of course, that you had memorised the entire deck but could only be bothered, or only had time, to recount half of them.

So, as has been shown, it is possible to do away with our host's marked cards and memorise a deck of cards *for real*. However, I will concede, that our host's method is both ingenious and far easier to master! You must decide for yourself which route you wish to take...

Nous Continuons...

After a first course of oysters and cream of barley soup, where the talk had been excited and had centred around several marvellous stories of the feats human beings are capable of under the correct circumstances (Campbell the lawyer recounted a fascinating story of a mother who had single-handedly lifted a horse and carriage to rescue her daughter who had become trapped beneath the contraption), Jones asked, "So, what other wonders do you have to show us? Don't be shy, old man, we are all quite captivated now by your odd little collection!"

"Well, if you're sure," I replied, "may I present to you Jack the Ripper's playing cards."

At the mention of Jack the Ripper, the widow Mrs. Hudson fainted dead away. She lay in a swoon upon the shag-pile carpet for several moments as my guests fussed around her, a thin line of saliva and cream of barley soup dribbling down her chin. I rang the bell for my butler George, and upon surmising the situation, he disappeared to return with smelling salts. Taking control of the situation, George soon had poor Mrs. Hudson returned to health. George had, at one point in his life, been an army doctor and so was used to dealing with medical emergencies such as Mrs.

Hudson's. The Belgian phrenologist Dr. De Ruysscher, I noted, did not rush forward to offer his services as a trained doctor, but rather loitered towards the back of the room, observing but not intervening. I began to wonder if the good doctor was really a doctor at all...

"Perhaps," I said, eyeing the somewhat battered and dilapidated playing cards, "this artefact is simply too much to demonstrate to such a gentle audience such this?"

"No, no!" exclaimed Mrs. Hudson, settling herself into a chair next to the fire and accepting the snifter of medicinal brandy offered to her by George. "Pray continue. I would not wish to spoil the evening. I am sure that if things get a little too excitable for me, I shall step outside to take the evening air."

"Very well," I acquiesced, and I picked up the playing cards that had once belonged to Jack the Ripper.

JACK THE RIPPER'S PICTURE BOOK

"A collector offered me these particular playing cards," I continued, "claiming that they had once belonged to the infamous Jack the Ripper. Or at least, he claimed, they were found close to the body of one of his victims, and they exhibited some strange tendencies when handled in a certain manner. At first I was dubious. My naturally sceptical mind was inclined to disbelieve the story being told to me and regard the collector as a charlatan intent on robbing me of my hard earned money in return for a simple pack of old playing cards. However, what he demonstrated to me encouraged me to believe him, and convinced me to hand over a not unsubstantial amount of money to purchase the cards."

I took the playing cards from their battered box, regarded them for a moment, and then continued, "If one card within a whole deck of playing cards could be said to represent the fiendish Jack the Ripper, surely it must be the Jack of Spades." From within the deck I fished out the Jack of Spades and held it before me for my guests to observe. "Firstly, the name. Jack. That is simple enough. However, let us consider the suit – Spades. The word 'spade' originates from the Italian word for a sword or knife – *spada*. So here we have the Jack of Knives. The Whitechapel Butcher. The Cutter."

Poor Mrs. Hudson looked fit to swoon once more, so I bit my tongue, smiled gently, and continued.

"However, there are other cards that may be said to represent certain characters who each played a role within the tragic tale of the Whitechapel murders. Several of the victims for instance may be said to be represented by certain cards. For example, poor Mary Jane Kelly, the final victim, the one left so mutilated by the fiend that her body was all but unrecognisable, could be represented by the Queen of Hearts, and perhaps the first victim, Polly Nichols, by the Queen of Diamonds. And the detectives – well let us say that the King of Clubs and the King of Spades may represent the detectives Abberline and McWilliam, the men who so famously failed to apprehend the notorious Jack.

"All of this sounds like fanciful conjecture of course, and when these notions were first pointed out to me I was as dismissive as perhaps you are now. But if I may beg your indulgence, I would like to demonstrate to you something very... *odd.*"

I placed the playing cards on the table and instructed the Belgian phrenologist De Ruysscher, who was seated next to me, to cut the cards in half. This he duly did. Then I asked him to turn the packet he had taken from the top of the deck face up and then place this face up packet on top of the remaining face down cards, so that essentially the pack of cards now consisted of half the pack face down and half face up.

I further instructed him to cut the cards again, but to cut deeper this time, perhaps ¾ of the way into the deck. He was then instructed to turn this new packet face up, and again place the packet onto the remaining face down deck.

With this task completed, I began to deal off one-by-one the face up cards which lay on top of the deck. As I did so I commented upon the occasional face up card. "Ah, the Queen of Hearts, poor dear Mary Jane Kelly. And here the King of Clubs, Detective Abberline perhaps. The 5 of Clubs, the number five representing the number of official victims, and here a deuce which reminds us of the two murders that took place on the 30th September 1888, those of Elizabeth Stride and Catherine Eddowes, the so-called *Double Event*."

Eventually I came to the first face down card in the pack. "All of these details are known," I said indicating to the face up cards that I had dealt off the top of the pack. "We know the victims, we know the detectives, we know the dates. The one thing we do not know is the motive, the reasoning, and the name. Who was Jack the Ripper? Will we ever know? Perhaps not. I fear that the identity of the killer will always be hidden, much like this first face down card that you, Dr. De Ruysscher , fairly cut to."

I turned over the face down card. It was the Jack of Spades. "Ah yes," I said, "as usual. The killer reveals himself through his playing cards, but we are none the wiser as to the identity of this Jack, the Jack of Knives, the Ripper."

A silence fell upon my guests and a chill air seemed to permeate the room. The silence was broken only by the sound of Mrs. Hudson hitting the shag-pile carpet face first, having once again collapsed into a swoon.

"Perhaps, in hindsight, brandy was not such a good idea, sir," said my butler, George. "Might I suggest a mug of beef tea for the lady?"

I leant forward in my chair and addressed De Ruysscher. "What would you prescribe, good doctor?" I asked of him. "Beef tea?"

"Ah, yes," he replied hesitantly. "Beef tea, by all means."

*

Our Host's Secret

This routine utilises a technique known in magical circles as the 'cut deeper' force. Allow me to quickly outline the mechanics once again. If you are unfamiliar with the devilish ways of the magician, it may prove helpful to have a deck of cards in your hands and follow along as I describe this technique.

Take a deck of cards and hold them in the normal manner as though ready to deal. The cards will, naturally, be face down so no-one can see the value of the cards. In this demonstration you are going to need the top card (the first face down card at the top of the deck) to be the Jack of spades. Bear this in mind for a moment.

Next you are going to turn the cards over and begin randomly dealing through them and perhaps placing cards down on the table. While you are doing this, you are discussing the meaning of several of the cards (Queen of Hearts = Mary Jane Kelly etc.) as demonstrated in my own exhibition during the dinner party. During this 'discussion' of the meaning of the cards in relation to Jack the Ripper folk lore, you are given ample opportunity to locate the Jack of spades, and as you gather the cards up to begin the 'magical' element of this performance, you need to ensure that the Jack of Spades is placed at the top of the deck (the first face down card in a deck held in the normal manner, as if ready for dealing).

Place the cards on the table and have a volunteer cut the deck in half. The top packet (just cut from the pack) is then to be turned face up and then replaced on top of the remaining face down cards. At this point you will have approximately half the pack face down (the bottom half of the deck) and half the pack face up (the top half).

Have the volunteer cut the deck of cards again, this time cutting slightly more than half-way (you will need to request this of the volunteer – instruct them as to what to do), and have this packet also turned face up and placed on top of the remaining deck.

Next, begin dealing card by card through the deck, these cards will all be face up, commenting on the various cards and mentioning any association we may have given them to the tale of Jack the Ripper. Eventually you will come to the first face down card. The mechanics of this trick mean that the first face down card you will encounter will be the card that was on top of the deck originally. In our case, the Jack of Spades. With much theatrics and aplomb, you turn over this card, reveal it to be the Jack of Spades, the Ripper card, and explain how this happens with eerie regularity with the deck of cards claimed to be once owned by the nefarious Jack the Ripper!

In essence, that is the cut deeper force.

However, I must reinforce the point that in this demonstration the subtleties employed mean that the first set of face up cards that we encounter have meaning and should not be lightly dismissed. We are hoping to weave a story around these face up cards, and they should be used to embellish the story of Jack the Ripper, and not rushed through to get to the 'big finish'.

Any 2 card (2 of Hearts, 2 of Spades, etc.) should prompt you to mention what is known as the 'double event'. This refers to September 30th 1888, when Elizabeth Stride and Catherine Eddowes were both murdered.

Any 5 card should prompt you to mention the 5 official victims of Jack the Ripper - Mary Ann Nichols, Annie Chapman, Elizabeth Stride, Catherine Eddowes, and Mary Jane Kelly.

Any King card should prompt you to mention Detective Abberline, the Scotland Yard detective put in charge of the case.

An Ace card should prompt you to mention the first official victim, Mary Ann Nichols.

The Queen of Hearts should prompt you to mention perhaps Mary Jane Kelly or indeed any of the victims. The same is true of the Queen of Diamonds and the Queen of Clubs.

I would use the Queen of Spades to mention the conspiracy theory that states that Jack the Ripper was indeed a woman. This theory is known as Jill the Ripper. A little on-line research with furnish you with ample details, should you desire them.

This routine obviously works best with an old pack of cards. If you use cards on a regular basis, I'm sure you will have a pack somewhere that is several years old and is not used anymore because they are getting a bit tatty. These cards are perfect.

Alternatively, carry a pack of cards around in your pockets for a few weeks, let them get beaten and battered, and they will soon start to resemble what a genuine pack of

Victorian playing cards would look like, or at the very least, what your audience will *believe* a genuine deck of cards from Victorian times would look like.

Another subtlety you might like to employ is to write the names of the victims on the Queen cards, and perhaps some names of the other main players in the drama on other royal cards, and explain how it is believed that Jack the Ripper used these very playing cards to document his adventures. Perhaps the playing cards acted as a kind of 'diary' in which he recorded his dark adventures? The writing should be appropriately menacing and dark, as though written by a man in the depths of emotional turmoil. Or, it strikes me as I recite these words, would a more elegant hand prove to be yet more sinister? Let your own imagination guide you...

*

Sherlock Holmes Says...

While our host has no doubt recounted a most ingenious method of enthralling your dinner guests, I must say that the notion of using the exploits of the world's most infamous murderer as a vehicle for entertainment strikes me as a little crass. However, I will concede that such gory tales do hold a certain fascination for the masses, as the popularity of Watson's sensationalised recollections of my own small adventures serves to illustrate only too well.

All the same, I do feel compelled to point out to the reader that Jack the Ripper was a real person, and his victims were real people too. It is easy to forget this when we are being regaled by Gothic tales of London fog, cobblestones, and sinister figures bathed in shadow.

So shrouded in myth and mystery is this story that the facts are hard to identify now that so many years have passed, and it is with certainty that I state that the true identity of Jack the Ripper shall never be known or revealed with any degree of certainty.

However, over the years sleuths of both a professional and amateur nature have attempted to unravel the truth. Of all the suspects put forward by these investigators, two names stand out for me. These are Kosminski, a poor Polish Jew resident in Whitechapel, and Dr Francis J. Tumblety, an American 'quack' doctor, who was arrested in November 1888 for offences of gross indecency, and fled the country later the same month, having obtained bail at a very high price.

Kosminski was the favoured suspect of Dr. Robert Anderson, the head of C.I.D. (Criminal Investigation Department), and the officer in charge of the case, Chief Inspector Donald Swanson.

Tumblety was stated to have been a chief suspect at the time of the murders and 'to my mind a very likely one,' by the ex-head of the Special Branch at Scotland Yard in 1888, ex-Detective Chief Inspector John George Littlechild. He relayed these suspicions in a letter to the noted criminologist, journalist, and author George R. Sims, in a letter dated 23rd September, 1913.

Following the police investigations of the time and subsequent analysis of the crimes, the commonly-held belief is that there are five 'official' victims of the Ripper. These are known as the *canonical* victims:

Mary Ann 'Polly' Nichols, murdered on Friday 31 August 1888.

Annie Chapman, murdered on Saturday 8 September 1888.

Elizabeth Stride, murdered on Sunday 30 September 1888.

Catherine Eddowes, also murdered on Sunday 30 September 1888.

Mary Jane Kelly, murdered on Friday 9 November 1888.

Other murders took place in the East End of London around the same time, let us not forget that both the area and the era were violent in the extreme, and it is held by some that a number of these murders, most particularly the murder of Martha Tabram on Tuesday, 7th August, 1888, are likely to have been the work of Saucy Jack. But, truth be told, we shall never know.

Perhaps the single reason for the enduring appeal of this sad tale of murder and prostitution is the rather flamboyant name of the perpetrator, Jack the Ripper. This name, a name known throughout the world, was signed at the end of a letter, dated 25th September, 1888, and received by the Central News Agency on 27th September, 1888. The Central News Agency, in turn, forwarded it to the Metropolitan Police on the 29th September. The letter began *'Dear Boss...'* and went on to describe the actions of the murderer in lurid detail. The signed name of Jack the Ripper was then made public, published in the newspapers of the day who covered the murders with gory enthusiasm, and the name became lodged in the imagination of the world.

These then are the facts that are known regarding Jack the Ripper, and in closing I would reiterate that the poor, unfortunate victims were real people, real women who may have been down on their luck, but who did not deserve the grisly end that they met. And Jack the Ripper, he was a real person, a male in all probability, who deserved to be caught and hung on the end of a rope for his crimes. Sadly, he evaded such justice, but let us hope that somehow, in some way, he was made to pay for his deeds.

*

Nous Continuons...

Mrs. Hudson was taken home in a hansom cab. It was agreed to be the best course of action for one so frail and easily overcome by excitable emotions, and my remaining guests enjoyed a main course of lamb, mint sauce, new potatoes and green peas.

"Playing cards are strange things," I observed to the assembled diners. "It is almost as though they are capable of acquiring thoughts, emotions, and memories from their human owners. Of course Gypsies have used them for several centuries as a tool of divination and fortune telling, and the Church has tried on more than one occasion to have them banned forever! Their association with gambling, cheating, necromancy, and illicit behaviour has led many to dub them 'the devil's picture book'. My collection contains, as you have already witnessed, several sets of cards. Perhaps if we have time, we shall return to them again."

"Have you more to show us?" asked Miss Carriger, flicking a guilty look at her mother, the redoubtable Mrs. Carriger. "I must confess to be thoroughly enjoying your demonstrations. They speak to me of a world of high adventure and excitement!"

"My dear!" exclaimed her mother through a mouthful of lamb. "Contain yourself! Do not badger your host so!"

"Oh please," I said, "it is no trouble at all. I do enjoy displaying my collection and will happily demonstrate another of my odd artefacts. Perhaps we can experience another strange occurrence before dessert is served?"

"Oh, yes, please do!" squealed Miss Carriger, clapping her hands together.

SEANCE FOR A CLOCK-MAKER

"There was once," I began, "an old clock-maker who resided in the Spitalfields area of London, not too far from the streets and alleyways where our old friend Jack the Ripper plied his nefarious trade. This clock-maker was a kindly old soul, much loved and admired by all for his craftsmanship, his jolly demeanour, and his charitable spirit.

"He owned a shop, of course, and inside could be found all manner of clock. Cuckoo clocks to rival the best that Switzerland has to offer, grandfather clocks that would not be out of place in the finest stately homes of England, and pocket watches that kept regimental time and helped countless factories and railways keep to their timetables.

"But the clock-maker's speciality was miniature grandfather and grandmother clocks. These tiny reproductions were dubbed grandchild clocks, and were designed to fit on mantelpieces and dressing tables – perfect copies in every way of their larger cousins.

"I have here a pendulum from one of these exquisite creations. See how perfect and delightful it is?" I held up a pendulum for all to see. "Although the clocks themselves were designed to be perfect reproductions of the far larger grandfather clocks, the pendulums that powered the mechanisms were often, like this, far more elaborate. The small clocks were ostensibly purchased by or for ladies, and so the clock-maker had a habit of producing these delicate, enchanting pendulums for them."

I handed the pendulum, with its intricate gold chain and crystal '*bob*', around the table for my guests to observe at close hand.

"Quite delightful," remarked Miss Carriger.

"Indeed," I agreed, taking the pendulum back. "Sadly the story of the clock-maker does not have a happy ending. One evening a gang of young ruffians broke their way into the shop. Finding the gentle clock-maker immersed in his work, they struck him about the body and demanded that he hand over money. The clock-maker was not a wealthy man, he was a craftsman not a businessman, and he informed these thugs that there was no money on the establishment. With this the ruffians flew into a fury and beat the poor defenceless clock-maker to death. The final blow was struck by one of his beautiful grandchild clocks, picked up and used as a hammer to the head."

This announcement was met by gasps of outrage from my assembled company. "Shameful!" bellowed Jones, the undertaker.

"This pendulum," I held the pendulum up and observed it, "was the pendulum located within the mechanics of the death dealing clock. It is funny, is it not, that something so small and so pretty could have such a gruesome history.

"The police did not require the services of a '*consulting detective*' to solve the riddle of who had murdered the old clock-maker. They found the ruffians in a near-by public house, drunk on cheap gin, boasting of their actions, and attempting to sell cuckoo clocks and pocket watches to the other drinkers.

"They were arrested, convicted, and duly hung by the neck until dead. And there, perhaps, the sad story should end. But no. Because something strange was observed by a relative of the clock-maker when he was in the process of organising the sale and disposal of the clock-maker's earthly possessions. I wonder if I may hand the pendulum to you, Miss Carriger?"

Miss Carriger, earlier delighting in the simple beauty of the pendulum, now regarded it with some suspicion. However, she obediently took the pendulum from me. I asked her to stand, demonstrated to her how to hold the pendulum, and called for the room to be hushed.

At my instruction George the butler extinguished the gas-lamps and the room fell into semi-darkness, illuminated only by a handful of candles. All eyes fell on Miss Carriger, holding the pendulum out before her.

"Clock-maker?" I whispered, regarding the pendulum. "Clock-maker? Hear me, clock-maker. Tick... *tock*, tick... *tock*, tick... *tock*."

Slowly yet surely, the pendulum began to move. Gently at first, but gathering strength as the seconds passed, the pendulum began to swing, backwards and forwards. The motion was eerie, other-worldly, as though the hand holding the pendulum no longer belonged to Miss Carriger, the pendulum itself taking on a ghostly glow as candle-light flickered on the crystal bob.

"Tick... *tock,*" I continued. "Tick... *tock...*"

Miss Carriger looked fascinated yet terrified, unable to tear her eyes from the pendulum as the swinging motion gathered strength and intensity. She appeared to be holding her breath, and she did not blink.

"It is a fascinating thing," I turned and whispered to my captivated guests. "It is as though the spirit of the clock-maker is imbued within the pendulum itself."

After a few moments more, I gently whispered into the ether, "Thank you clock-maker, but please, now, step away from Miss Carriger. Stop the pendulum, step away."

And surely enough, the pendulum came to a gentle halt. There were muffled gasps from my guests, and Miss Carriger placed a hand to her mouth, unsure whether to giggle nervously or cry out in awe. I took the pendulum from her and she slumped in her chair.

"Well I never!" exclaimed her mother, Mrs. Carriger. "How intriguing!"

Our Host's Secret

Pendulums have been used for hundreds, perhaps thousands, of years and have a number of uses. They have been employed in dowsing, to perhaps locate underground streams of water or precious minerals, and they have often been used by those of a spiritual nature to communicate with so-called *spirits* and *ghosts*.

A pendulum is essentially a short length of string or chain, at the end of which is placed a weight. This weight can be as simple as a stone, or as ornate as a crystal. When the pendulum is held at the string or chain end between the index finger and thumb, with the arm outstretched, it is possible to make the pendulum swing in order to answer questions. The volunteer will not feel that they are making the pendulum swing, it will appear to the volunteer and those watching that the pendulum is moving of its own volition.

Some people attach an *esoteric* explanation as to why a pendulum would moving seemingly by itself. They believe it is the spirits communicating with us, or some other ethereal energy acting upon the instrument. However, I am more inclined, being of an analytical nature, to believe that the pendulum moves because of something called *ideomotor phenomenon.* Ideomotor phenomenon states that the human body is never truly at rest. It is always moving, even in the slightest degree. It is these tiny movements, perhaps combined with an element of wish-fulfilment, that encourages the pendulum to gently begin swinging. Ideomotor phenomenon is also used to explain the movement of the pointer (the *planchette*) on a so-called Ouija board.

As always with this kind of demonstration, choosing a good volunteer is essential. A demonstration of the pendulum is not as fool proof as, say, the use of a marked deck of cards! But with a little thought and common-sense, a good volunteer can always be found. I genuinely feel that if the surroundings, the atmosphere, and the expectation are in place, any person can become an ideal candidate for this kind of demonstration.

If you come from a magical background and have never used a pendulum routine, I would encourage you to embrace the uncertainty, the unknown, and the excitement that a pendulum can bring. The magic takes place in the volunteer's hand. Perhaps it is this simple fact that makes pendulums so powerful. And if you, from whatever background you are approaching this from, have never seen a pendulum is action, please treat yourself to a pendulum (they are readily available on-line or from any local *New Age* or *hippy* shops), and try it out on yourself. Simply hold the pendulum aloft and will it to move. You will be as amazed as dear Miss Carriger was when the damnable thing just begins to swing by itself!

From a personal point of view, in this particular demonstration, I would tend to use a small crystal pendulum as one can imagine such an object being used as the clock pendulum in a miniature clock designed for a woman's dressing table. Although, of course, any pendulum will suffice.

I find with this routine that the more gently I speak to encourage the pendulum to move, the better results I observe. Gently whispering "tick... *tock*" with a slightly different emphasis on the *tock* yields far better results that calling out, "Move the pendulum! Make the pendulum move!" It is also far creepier as well. Less is more, and all that.

*

Sherlock Holmes Says...

Grandchild clocks have existed perhaps for as long as there have been the larger and grander *grandfather* and *grandmother* clocks. There will always be debate on these matters, but the history of this style of clock can certainly and reliably be traced back to the 17th Century.

Although less well known than their larger counterparts, grandchild clocks (sometimes known as granddaughter clocks) are *bona fide* items, although I fear that our host has taken some liberties in their description. They were a little larger than he outlines, being traditionally sized around four to five feet in height. Certainly they would be too large to sit upon a lady's mantelpiece or dressing table as described by our host!

However, I do find the notion of these tiny clocks with their elaborate pendulums to be quite an enchanting idea, and so, on this occasion if nowhere else, I would not be minded to let historical accuracy get in the way of a good yarn!

*

Nous Continuons...

George, the butler, sidled up to me discreetly and inquired if I was ready for the dessert to be served. I looked across the table at Miss Carriger, still talking excitedly about her pendulum experience, and noted the giddy twinkle in her eye. Her imagination had been piqued, and no doubt.

"Hold off for five minutes if you would, George my man," I said. "Give me chance to press home my advantage."

I winked at the butler, who nodded knowingly and left the room.

"I say!" I called across to Miss Carriger. "My butler informs me that dessert has been delayed by five minutes. I do apologise for the kitchen's tardiness, but I wonder if we might not employ this short demurral to engage in another amusement?"

"Oh, of course!" agreed Miss Carriger.

"Whatever next?" said Campbell, the lawyer. "I'm not sure my old ticker can handle all this drama!"

"I think this quick demonstration may be equally of interest to the gentlemen as to the ladies," I said. "There is a scientific quality to this item that may appeal to your analytic mind, Campbell, and to you Dr. De Ruysscher. Your studies in phrenology may mean you will have some unique input to offer us."

"Well, consider me intrigued," sniffed the lawyer.

"Pray continue," smiled the Belgian doctor. "I too have had my interest piqued."

THE SHERLOCK HOLMES PERSONALITY PROFILING SYSTEM

I produced a regular, average deck of cards and introduced them to my guests.

"We have used playing cards already tonight, and you might recall that I have already commented on the strange nature of these items. How they can be regarded as instruments of the devil, how they can become imbued with human emotion, how they are used for gambling and fortune telling. But playing cards can also be used as windows into the very human soul."

"How so?" demanded Jones, the undertaker, looking decidedly unconvinced.

"Well," I said, "you will have, I'm sure, heard of the work of Sigmund Freud and his associates? His work into psychoanalysis, an attempt to understand and interpret the unconscious mind, dreams, and anxieties?"

Jones *harrumphed* to indicate that although he had indeed heard of Freud, he did not altogether approve of him. De Ruysscher smiled and nodded his head vigorously, letting me know that he was well aware of Freud's work and looked upon it more favourably than perhaps Jones did.

"I am sure that Dr Joseph Bell, up until his sad demise in 1911, would have been most fascinated by the work of

Freud, and I am certain that Holmes, had he been an actual person rather than a figment of Doyle's imagination, would have been only to keen to incorporate Freud's work into his own.

"Let us examine these playing cards, for instance," I continued. "Such a simple design, and yet what secrets could be hidden within the four suits, the fifty-two cards, and their numbers?"

I handed the deck to Miss Carriger.

"Please," I said, "if you would be so kind, could you fan through the cards and pick out one card from each suit. One heart, one spade, one club, and one diamond. Do this quite at random, do not think too deeply about it, but ensure that you look at all fifty-two cards before making your decision."

Miss Carriger duly took the cards in her hands and looked through them. She fumbled on occasion, excusing herself for being so clumsy, but I reassured her and she went about her task with enthusiasm. After a few moments she placed down four cards upon the title, one card from each suit, a Heart, a Spade, a Club, and a Diamond. I placed the cards, face up in a line upon the table so that all could see them quite plainly.

The cards chosen were the Queen of Hearts, the 2 of Clubs, the 9 of Diamonds, and the 10 of Spades.

"Quite fascinating," I whispered.

"How so?" enquired Miss Carriger, a gentle smile quivering across her lips.

I looked around the table at my assembled guests and I smiled.

"I asked Miss Carriger to choose four cards, one from each suit, completely at random. But the fact of the matter is that there is no such thing as a random act. At all stages the unconscious mind is at work, directing our actions, influencing us in ways that we are only just coming to understand. Miss Carriger's conscious mind may have believed that she was choosing these playing cards completely at random, but in reality her hand was guided by her unconscious mind, and as such her choices can tell us a lot about who she is, what motivates her, and what she wants from life."

"I say," said Campbell, "is it quite decent? All this talk of the unconscious mind and motivations? Is it meant for polite company?"

"My dear Campbell," I said, "it is perfectly decent. It is *science*, for goodness sakes! But you are right, it is knowledge that should be used wisely. It should not have been seen as a mere frippery."

I turned to Miss Carriger and, indicating the cards that lay on the table before her, asked, "Would you be so kind as to allow me to interpret your cards in front of our guests? To examine who you are and what motivates you?"

Before her daughter could answer, the mother chimed in, "Well, I'm not entirely sure that this is a suitable..."

"Of course!" proclaimed the daughter, stopping her mother mid-pronouncement. "I would be delighted!"

Her eyes flickered momentarily towards her mother, and then returned their gaze to me.

"Very well," I said, and I began.

"You chose four cards, one from each suit. Let us examine the suits firstly. Each of the four suits could be said to represent one aspect of life, of human existence as it were. The Hearts, well that is easy. Hearts represent love, relationships, our family and our friends," I waved an arm around the table. "Diamonds, however, could be said to represent more material aspects of life. Money, possessions, even the work that men engage in.

"Spades may be said to represent the changes we want to make in life. You may recall I described how the word *spades* comes from the Italian word for sword, so we can imagine a sword cutting through dead wood, and effecting changes in our life.

"And Clubs, well, Clubs represent no less than our dreams and our hopes, our very desires in life. You may have seen the amusing cartoons in Punch magazine where characters are talking or thinking to themselves, and often-times these thoughts or words are placed in bubbles above their heads," Miss Carriger smiled to confirm that she had indeed enjoyed such amusements. "Well, how like the emblem for the Clubs suit do those thought bubbles look? And so we may imagine that the Clubs represent our dreams and our hopes, those thought we keep to ourselves.

"And now comes the interesting part," I continued. "Which cards, which numbers, within the various suits did you choose? Firstly, the Queen of Hearts. This card shows you, Miss Carriger, as a warm, caring, loving person. You literally see yourself as a Queen of Hearts, taking care of those you love, your family and your friends, whilst also relishing the feeling of being cared for and nurtured in return." I turned to her mother. "Congratulations on raising such a loving and caring child," I said, "who now blossoms into a young lady in her own right."

Mrs. Carriger forced a sour smile onto her face, unable to mask the fact that she did not approve of this *psychoanalysis* of her daughter taking place. I continued regardless.

"Secondly, the 2 of Clubs. The two is a very low number, and this indicates to me that you do not have much faith that you will be able to achieve your goals or attain your dreams. A high number, a nine or a ten or one of the royal cards, would have indicated to me that you are bristling with optimism, that you felt your dreams were within grasp. But a low number, that sadly shows to me that you feel you may never achieve those things you dream of. Let us move on...

"The 9 of Diamonds, however, indicates that you do enjoy the finer things that life has to offer. Nice clothes, good food, even, dare I say it, fine wine. You enjoy and appreciate the finer aspects of life, and there is nothing wrong with that at all. For what is the point of wealth if one cannot take the time to appreciate it?

"And finally the 10 of Spades. Ten is a high number, so I am minded to say that you wish to make some changes in your life. A low number in this aspect would indicate that you feel unable to make changes. However, such a high number would tell me that you are hopeful of making some important changes in your life, and I wish you well in this endeavour. You are indeed a most intriguing young lady, Miss Carriger, and I wish you well in all your endeavours."

The table sat in silence for a moment. Miss Carriger stared at me intently, and then, with a single tear rolling from her eye and down her cheek, she said, "Sir, it is like you have a window through which you can observe my very soul."

*

Our Host's Secret

Really, there is no trick to this little demonstration. Rather it is the application of common sense.

If one accepts, as I do, that the unconscious mind is always gently steering the conscious mind in whatever direction it believes is the most favourable for the individual, then one must also accept that there is no such thing as a 'random choice'. The unconscious mind always dictates what form that randomness should take, like an unseen, silent mentor.

With this premise accepted, a deck of cards ceases to be a collection of images, colours, and numbers, but rather a road-map by which one can decipher the personality of an individual.

Miss Carriger was asked to choose four seemingly random cards, one from each suit. The suits themselves are relatively easily to assign a meaning to: Hearts meaning love, relationships, friendships and family, Diamonds representing money, work, and the material things in life, Spades talk of change, of people cutting through the *dead wood* in their lives and effecting changes, while Clubs are about dreams, desires, and the goals that people would like to see themselves achieving.

With these four rudimentary meanings associated to the four suits of the deck of cards, the next step is to associate meanings to the number. Again, this has an almost childlike simplicity to it. The higher the number, the more positive a person sees themselves in that area.

A low number such as a 2 or 3 talks of someone lacking in confidence in that area, they are struggling to see that subject in a positive light.

The more 'middle-of-the-road' numbers such a 4, 5, and 6 indicate that this person feels in a reasonably healthy position when it comes to this particular area.

The higher numbers, from 7 up to 10, show the person feeling progressively more positive in that area. A 7 would indicate healthy optimism, while a 10 would represent someone who was brimming with confidence and excitement when it comes that this subject.

The royal cards are interesting. They are clearly positive, up-beat cards. But they can often be a mirror representing the person who has chosen the cards.

If a female chooses a Queen, this can indicate that they see that area being of particular importance to them, and they feel as though they are in control when it comes to making decisions in that area.

Likewise, for a Jack and a King for a male. While the King may be a card of silent confidence, of mastery and control, the Jack may be more likely to represent excitement, risk taking, and adventure (think of the Jack of Hearts running away with the tarts!).

The Ace can have a dual meaning. Often in card games, the Ace can represent 1 or 10. Likewise when using the cards to interpret someone's personality, the Ace can demonstrate a duality in that person's personality. They can sometimes be lacking confidence to an acute degree, while other times they can be full of energy and excitement for the given subject. They can change their mind or their outlook in a moment, and this contrariness may be a large part of their nature.

With just a little imagination and thought, I am sure that you, dear reader, can see how a simple deck of playing cards can become a potent tool in the area of personality profiling.

Try it out on your friends and see how fascinating it can be, but also be prepared to be inundated with requests from others around you who would like their personality profiling also!

*

Sherlock Holmes Says...

I will, shortly, discuss the psycho-mumbo-jumbo that our gracious host has just attempted to describe. However, I thought that, firstly, it would be far more entertaining to examine the peculiar habits of Freud (I believe our host alluded to him some moments previously), and see how they correspond to my own.

The interesting fact is that Freud was in the 1880s, like myself, a cocaine user. One must recall that at the time cocaine was not prohibited by the law, and was often prescribed and used as a euphoric. The more harmful side of the drug had not yet been investigated or acknowledged.

It is fascinating to recall that popular drinks such as the ubiquitous Coca-Cola once contained cocaine! First produced in 1886, it wasn't until 1929 that Coca-Cola would be completely free of cocaine. Cocaine addiction and the harmful side-effects of cocaine use were therefore only fully understood later.

Like myself, Freud used cocaine as a stimulus, something to help him manage his depression, and achieve a state of wellbeing. For myself, I can only say that I needed stimulation for my *over-active* brain in periods when I did not have interesting cases to solve, and I deduce that Freud's use of the drug was for very similar reasons as my own.

Of course, had we known of the detrimental side-effects of cocaine use, I am sure that we would have both made very different choices. I should also point out that Watson did try to deter me from use, and in this instance, if no other, he was entirely correct.

Moving on to the psycho-babble of analysing the personality of another. The idea of analysing, or *reading*, an individual's personality in the manner prescribed by our host, rather than being a genuine attempt at unravelling unconscious motivations, is often described, by more cynical folk, as 'cold reading'.

The term 'cold reading' indicates that one is *reading* a personality *cold* – as in, with no previous knowledge. Cold reading is quite a fascinating subject in itself, and had I more time I might find myself researching the subject in greater depth. However, I have done *some* research, which I think it would be advantageous to share with you.

Where does cold reading as a technique originate? Well, let me take you on a little journey through time and space. Let us board an imaginary time machine and travel forwards in time, from London in the year 1922 to the Mid-West of the United States in the 1930s.

At that future time, large carnivals would travel from town to town, putting on circus shows and presenting sideshow attractions for the local populace before, after a few days, moving on to the next town.

These carnivals would both fascinate and infuriate the townsfolk of the locations visited. On the one hand those who worked in the carnivals were generally seen as thieves, con-men, and ne'er-do-wells. But on the other hand, who could resist the lure of the bright lights, the smell of the candy-floss, and the dubious delights of such attractions as the *Bearded Lady* and the *Man-Eating Chicken*?

An integral part of the carnival would be the palm reader's tent (known colloquially as the 'mitt camp', mitt referring to the hand). The palm reader was generally female and would dress appropriately for her role, dressing in a manner that would be seen as mysterious and gypsy-like. Her tent likewise would be covered in moons and stars, and the inside would be dark and candle-lit.

The interested customer would enter the tent, cross the palm reader's hand with silver, and would then receive their 'reading', the palm reader being able to discern with amazing accuracy the personality traits of the customer, and also describe past events and predict the future.

The carnival palm reader however would not be genuinely psychic or blessed with any esoteric knowledge. For the most part, the palm reader was employing a technique known as 'The Spiel'.

The Spiel was a standard piece of patter that was handed down orally from one generation of carnival palm readers to another. The Spiel was a script, a script that would be used for each and every customer who entered the tent. Every customer would essentially be receiving the same reading.

The Spiel, the script employed, would be full of stock phrases. These stock phrases would be along the lines of: 'you can sometimes be the life and soul of the party yet other times you find yourself in a more reflective mood'. The stock phrase is designed to sound very specific, but it is in fact a statement that would be generally true of each and every person.

The Spiel also used a technique whereby each statement contained both positive and negative elements, so for example 'you are sometimes the life of the party but other times you aren't', or perhaps 'you know you are a good person but sometimes you have doubts about things you have done in the past'. This means that, although the statement sounds specific and full of wisdom, it is in fact a fail-safe phrase. It cannot fail as it contains both an initial declaration and then its counterpart.

So each and every person receiving The Spiel was essentially being fed the same script. This would work well for 3 very good reasons:

1. The Spiel utilises an under-appreciated fact that Human Beings are more alike than they are different. People have a tendency to go through life fooling themselves that they are uniquely individual and that nobody else on the face of the planet is like them. The rather humbling truth is that Human Beings are all the same. They all experience the same emotions, the same ups and downs in life. The life of your friend and neighbour is likely to be little different from your own.

2. People misremember situations to a ridiculously high degree. Two people witnessing the same bank robbery or street-mugging will provide the police with two entirely different descriptions, right down to the colour of the

perpetrator's clothes and the number of crooks involved. This is a phenomenon well known to myself and to the law enforcement agencies. It is almost as though the mind takes in what little information it observes and then conjures up all the extraneous details for itself, over-riding the actual experience with thoughts and images based more on previous experiences, beliefs, and biases than genuine fact. Therefore, two people receiving The Spiel will report totally different experiences. By the time they leave the palm reader's tent, they will have rewritten the experience in their minds so that it become a uniquely individual experience.

3. And finally, once the palm reader has memorised The Spiel, her performances from that moment onwards could be described as *plain sailing*! She does not have to work hard trying to deliver a unique reading for every person who enters her tent. Rather, she can simply go into automatic mode and recite her script. Those who would work in the mitt camp were keen to make life as easy as possible for themselves! Who wants to work for a living?! But The Spiel is most certainly not cold reading, although many people believe it is. Let me explain.

The term cold reading actually refers to a skill that we all employ every day of our lives. Cold reading is literally reading somebody from cold.

When we see a stranger in the street we are unable to *not* make snap, irrational judgements about them (no matter how liberal and open-minded we fool ourselves that we are). We look at a stranger's clothes and make snap decisions about how wealthy and stylish we think they are. From their clothes we also make snap judgements about the person's life-style, their political persuasions, their religion (or lack of), etc. Combining the clothes with the physical attributes (attractiveness, weight, hair, etc.) we also make the most important of human decisions; do we find them attractive, do we think they could help us in life, and do we think we like them?

We make all these decisions usually within the first few seconds of meeting them, and indeed we make similar decisions almost instantaneously with people we pass on the stairs or who we walk past in the street. Once we add into the equation their voice and their mannerisms, within a matter of seconds we have decided whether or not we are going to like this person.

Once this irrational and totally judgemental decision has been made, it can take weeks or even months or years for someone who you internally decided you did not like to win you over and prove to you that actually they are actually a jolly decent chap! How many times have I personally heard the phrase, "When I first met you I didn't like you? But now I have changed my opinion and actually think that you are a good person!" Talk about a back-handed compliment! This is cold reading. The ability of the human to make snap decisions about people based purely on the way an individual looks and other such superficial details.

On top of cold reading, there are also techniques known as *warm reading* and *hot reading*. When talking about cold reading, I find that many armchair experts often mistakenly incorporate elements from these other techniques into their definition, so perhaps it is important that we cover these techniques also.

Warm reading is the technique that utilises the most elements from the original Spiel of the carnival palm readers. It is a set of phrases, often known as *Barnum Statements*, that are vague enough to apply to most people but sound very specific. They also contain the positive and negative elements discussed earlier, such as "sometimes you like to attend social functions, but at other times you do not".

Here then is a list of the accepted Barnum Statements, although of course there is nothing stopping a person from inventing a few of their own:

• You have a great need for other people to like and admire you.

• You have a tendency to be critical of yourself.

• You have a great deal of unused capacity which you have not turned to your advantage.

• While you have some personality weaknesses, you are generally able to compensate for them.

• Your sexual adjustment has presented problems for you.

• Disciplined and self-controlled outside, you tend to be worrisome and insecure inside.

• At times you have serious doubts as to whether you have made the right decision or done the right thing.

• You prefer a certain amount of change and variety and become dissatisfied when hemmed in by restrictions and limitations.

• You pride yourself as an independent thinker and do not accept others'

statements without satisfactory proof.

• You have found it unwise to be too frank in revealing yourself to others.

• At times you are extroverted, affable, sociable, while at other times you are introverted, wary, reserved.

• Some of your aspirations tend to be pretty unrealistic.

• Security is one of your major goals in life.

Let us now talk about hot reading. Hot reading is the technique of obtaining information about a person that you know to be correct, and then regurgitating this information during a reading.

In the 21st Century, I am led to believe, researching the traits, personality, and background of an individual is a relatively simple task, made all the easier by something that will, I understand, be known as the *Internet*. Within this so-called Internet are websites with such perplexing names as *Google* and *Facebook*. While I must admit that the intricacies of these devices is somewhat beyond my late 19th and early 20th Century understanding, I am led to believe that simply entering an individual's name and location can spew forth an incredible amount of information. How such a device would have aided me in my own investigations!

With such information at the finger-tips, it is then child's play to feed this knowledge back to the individual as if this knowledge is being obtained from cards or palm reading or the crystal ball placed atop the table.

In my days, pre-internet, riffling through a lady's purse, eaves-dropping on conversations, and bribing servants for *tit-bits* of information would have been just a few of the many underhand methods utilised by the fraudulent medium, psychic, or *reader*.

The combination of cold reading, warm reading, and hot reading is generally what is meant when people refer to the term 'cold reading'. There is also another element – experience.

As someone who, as a consulting detective, has been engaged in the darkest recesses of human life for most of my adult life, I have come to some quite sobering realisations about the masses. Generally, underneath the guise of niceness and respectability that most people demonstrate, Human Beings are decidedly selfish creatures. This selfishness may never manifest itself, and the person may live their life as a perfect saint, helping others, and never saying a cross word about anyone. However, I guarantee you, underneath the surface, in every person, there is a small child stamping its feet and shouting that life is not fair!

Even the most helpful, accommodating individual will, at some level, believe that they always get treated shabbily when compared to their counterparts. They will believe that they work harder than most people, that their work is tougher than anyone realises, and that other people generally get an easier ride than them.

Of course they realise that there is genuine hardship and horror in the world and that they are lucky to live without the fear and desperation that many experience in some parts of the globe. But in general, in their office, in their factory, in their home and neighbourhood, amongst friends and family, they believe that their life is harder and less rewarding than most.

At work, they are the most industrious and yet they get the least recognition. In the home, should they not be in a position to employ servants, they believe that it is always they that has to wash up the dirty dishes, cook the food for the table, put the children to bed, walk the dog around the streets etc., while everyone else in the household does less than them. Or they will believe that they have to work harder in their place of employment than other members of the household understand, and so they should be allowed to rest, put their feet up, and relax when they return to the homestead, rather than being badgered and berated.

This selfishness in most people will never or rarely manifest itself. In others it will be bubbling away constantly. The only difference between the polite member of society who is always prepared to help others and the angry man who is always shouting and complaining is that the polite person is better at hiding and controlling his inner spoilt child.

Therefore, mentioning in a reading that the person sitting before you works harder than most people realise and is not, in general terms, given the praise they deserve, will be met with almost universal approval. "Oh thank goodness, Mr. Holmes," they will exclaim, "you understand me so well!"

Another realisation, that I deduced following years of working in the field, is that there is a general formula that people tend to employ when thinking about the past, the present and the future (the bedrock of many of these so-called readings). It is a very simple equation: people believe that the past twelve months have been quite difficult with some ups and downs (think of that inner spoilt child again), they believe that right now in the present they have some difficult decisions to make, but once those decisions are made the future will be a lot brighter.

So in short, past = bad, present = decisions to be made, future = good.

I made the mistake many years ago of telling someone, whom I had analysed using my own methods of deduction, that the past year had been quite a productive and positive one. "Pah!" she exclaimed. "Positive?! The things I've had to put up with over the last year you wouldn't believe! It's been truly awful!"

I quickly realised that no matter what the actual truth might be, people tend to believe that the past year has been a time of trials and tribulations. There may have been some good elements, but in the main they will believe that it has been a period when it has been necessary to climb over some hurdles.

I believe that this is just another manifestation of the inner spoilt child believing that they get it worse than most others!

*

Nous Continuons...

With Miss Carriger's personality profiling completed, I turned my attention to our Belgian friend, the good doctor of phrenology.

"I say, De Ruysscher," I said, "while we await dessert, would you mind informing our guests of what it is that you exactly do? I'm sure we would all be most fascinated by the intricacies of phrenology, especially following all that we have witnessed thus far tonight?"

"Of course, my dear chap!" exclaimed the doctor, leaning forward in his chair. His English was perfect, but it was spoken with clipped continental tones. He took a few moments to light a cigar and then lent back in his chair, a plume of bluey-grey smoke enveloping him for a moment.

A PHRENOLOGIST SPEAKS...

"I was most interested," began De Ruysscher, "in your demonstration with the lovely Miss Carriger. Of course there are many routes we may take if we wish to open a window to the soul. Your use of playing cards was fascinating, but we could also have chosen dream interpretation, the palm reading favoured by gypsies, or even the analysis of tea-leaves left in the bottom of a cup!

"Some of these techniques, dare I say it, are more scientific in their approach than others, and the technique that I employ, and that has brought me a modicum of acclaim, is perhaps the most scientifically proven of all these various systems. It is known as phrenology."

He pronounced *phrenology* as though it were four separate words, phren-ol-o-gy, and waved a hand in the air as he did so, like a maestro conducting an orchestra.

"To put it quite simply," he continued, "phrenology is the study of the human cranium, or skull. The cranium is, of course, home to the brain, and the size and shape of the cranium can indicate to us the size, shape, and make-up of the brain. Phrenology states that the brain is made up of twenty-seven individual organs. Each of these organs controls certain aspects of the human personality, the intelligence, *et cetera, et cetera.*

"By examining the shape of the skull, it is possible to ascertain the nature and the personality of the individual. From the romantic poet to the back street murderer, all is controlled by the shape and make-up of the brain, and this can be seen by observing the shape and make-up of the skull."

"So what about old Jones here?" I smiled, looking over at the undertaker. "What observations can you make about him, based on his skull?"

Jones snorted his disapproval and was about to voice an objection, but De Ruysscher jumped in before him.

"Well normally, of course, I would do a lot of the *seeing* with my hands. It is normal practice in phrenology to examine the skull with the hands in order to get a full picture, and also to take quite extensive measurements so that an individual's cranium can be compared with previous samples. However, in such refined company, I dare say we can dispense with such a physical approach and I shall make my deductions based on observation alone."

De Ruysscher was silent for a moment. He placed a pair of *pince-nez* onto the tip of his nose and spent a full thirty seconds observing Jones, who clearly was not enjoying the attention. The whole room fell into reticence, and the ticking of the grandfather clock in the hallway was the only sound to be heard.

At length, the doctor removed the glasses from his nose and lent back in his chair. He addressed Jones, "Your skull, sir, is the perfect specimen of its kind."

Jones seemed unsure of whether to take this as a compliment or not. "How so?" was all he managed to stutter.

"You have a very, how do you English say it? *Down to earth* character? You are *salt of the earth*, a very practical man. You are a problem solver, an intelligent man who does not *suffer fools lightly!*" he said, exaggerating each turn of phrase with a flourish of the hand, as though the orchestra that he had previously been conducting were now reaching the climax of their performance.

"So not a man prone to take flights of fancy?" he asked.

"Most certainly not!" stated the doctor.

"Not a person with an excitable nature, or an over-active imagination?"

"No, no, no! Not at all!"

I leant back in my chair. Maybe there was something to this phrenology after all.

*

Sherlock Holmes Says...

Phrenology is doubtless a fascinating subject to study. I, myself, have taken a little time to learn what I could about the practice.

Phrenology was very popular during the early part of the 19th Century, and in Britain the centre for those interested in the subject was Edinburgh, where the Edinburgh Phrenological Society was established in 1820 by brothers George and Andrew Combe. The society could boast Charles Darwin as a member, alongside many other luminaries.

However, by the mid-19th Century, phrenology had largely been discredited as an exact science, and indeed the Edinburgh Phrenological Society's last meeting took place in 1870.

The reason that Dr. De Ruysscher is being entertained by the Royal Society in the year 1922, and has been able to carve out something of a reputation for himself, is that in the early 20th Century phrenology has undergone something of a renaissance. This is due in no small part to the popularity of crime novels, and stories about the exploits of so-called private detectives. I imagine that Watson's lurid tales of our own adventures, served up in the Strand magazine for a public enthralled by the cut and thrust of detective work, are somewhat to blame for this, and so, inadvertently, I may have inspired a resurgence in the study of phrenology.

Although I have a personal interest in the subject matter, I am aware that it cannot be regarded as an exact science, so I am unsure as how to regard this current level of interest. I am certain that it is not possible to judge a man's morality and his likelihood to commit crime purely by observing the shape and size of his head, and my main concern is the fear that a man may be falsely imprisoned, or even, perish the thought, executed, on the say-so of one of these self-styled phrenologists. Let us hope that as the 20th Century advances, common sense prevails and phrenology once more becomes merely a subject of interest rather than being regarded as a science.

*

Nous Continuons...

"What do you make of all that Cottingley fairy nonsense of a few years back?" bellowed Jones, the undertaker, wiping his mouth on a napkin, as we enjoyed a dessert of poached pears. "Your man Doyle was immersed in all that chicanery, wasn't he?"

"Indeed he was," I said. "Doyle is a fascinating character. On the one hand he created Sherlock Holmes, the very embodiment of deduction and logical thinking, while on the other hand he is a fervent Spiritualist and believes without doubt that the fairies of Cottingley were and continue to be real."

"Fairies!" snorted Jones. "Poppycock, what?!"

"Perhaps," I conceded. "Or perhaps not. I have some very interesting items to show you. Perhaps when we retire for coffee and cigars?"

"Fairies!" Jones snorted once more, shaking his head.

With the dining completed, the remaining ladies in our party, Miss Carriger and her mother, decided that the hour was growing late and so they set about saying their farewells; this decision inspired, I suspected, by Mrs Carriger's dislike for my earlier analysis of her daughter's psyche via the medium of playing cards.

Dr. De Ruysscher decided that he would escort the ladies to their cabs, and then take his own cab back to the Savoy Hotel, were he was ensconced during his stay in London.

I wished them all a happy new year and thanked the esteemed phrenologist for indulging us. They in turn thanked me for an enchanting evening, and Miss Carriger voiced her hope that I would demonstrate the strange attributes of other items in my collection for her and her mother at some later date. I, of course, agreed to do exactly that.

And so it was that at approximately 11pm on December 31st 1922, I found myself alone with the lawyer Campbell and the undertaker Jones for company.

George poured coffee and brandy for us, and I offered cigars to the gentlemen which were readily accepted. On the small table still lay the items from my collection, amongst them two small silver rings that hardly looked big enough to fit an adult's finger.

"So, Jones," I said, "the Cottingley fairies. An interesting story, do you not agree? On the one hand the rational *adult* mind in us dismisses the very notion. Impossible! Inconceivable! The tales emanating from Yorkshire must surely be nothing more than yarns, fables, and untruths! And yet when we look at the photographs, the ones published just lately in the Strand magazine, there is something *ethereal* about them that draws us in and we find ourselves, momentarily, believing."

"Pah!" laughed Jones. "You, maybe! But not me!"

"Well, perhaps we shall see," I smiled and approached the table.

THE CURIOUS CASE OF THE FAIRY RINGS

I picked up the two small, silver finger rings. They were quite plain in appearance and I toyed with them for a moment. Then I began, "At the height of the Cottingley *incident*, I took it upon myself to take the long train journey to Bradford in Yorkshire, and make my way to the small village of Cottingley which lays a few miles to the north of that great industrial city. With such an interest in Holmes, Doyle, and life's more mysterious side, I decided that I owed myself no less. My intention was to interview the family, talk to the two girls involved, and perhaps get to the bottom of this most perplexing case.

"When I arrived at number 31 Main Street, in the village of Cottingley, Arthur Wright, the father, was not best pleased to see me. I suspect that the attention of the press and the accompanying notoriety had quite placed a strain on his nerves.

"However common decency dictated that he at least welcome me into his home for a little sustenance before I returned to Bradford train station to embark on the long journey back to London. The weather was foul, rain was lashing down, dark clouds rumbling overhead, and I rather suspect that the dour old Yorkshireman took at least a little pity on me.

"Once I was seated in the kitchen, a cup of sweet hot tea in my hands and my over-coat drying by the stove, I noticed that I was being observed by two young girls from the kitchen doorway. Elsie and Frances no less, the girls who had taken the infamous photographs. They were quickly shooed away by the mother, and I was left alone in the kitchen with Arthur who watched over me like a prison guard, encouraging me to drink my tea and be on my way.

"However after a minute or two his demeanour relaxed just slightly. 'Bleedin' fairies!' he exclaimed to me in a thick Yorkshire brogue. 'I rue the day I ever set eyes on them photographs! Brought us nothin' but bad luck!'

"'Bad luck?' I enquired. 'How so?'

"He sighed heavily and began, 'The neighbours all laugh at us now or avoid us like we have the plague! But that's just the start. Now there's the journalists, poking around, asking questions, looking at me like I'm a moron. And all that's without mentioning the curious folk who just want to gawp at us and tell their friends that they've seen the fairy people. Mr. Doyle, he's nice enough, but I wish to goodness he'd just let the matter be. I wish for nothing more than to be left alone and for things to return to normal, whatever normal might actually be.'

"The man's gaze came to rest on two silver finger rings, designed for children if their size was anything to go by, resting on one of the kitchen work tops. He seemed to hesitate for a moment, then he snatched them up and blurted out, 'Do you want these? They're silver. Probably worth a bob or two. You can have them! Free of charge! A gift from me to you, on account of your troubles.'

"I didn't know quite what to say. How could I possibly accept such a gift? I asked him who the rings belonged to and where they came from. The man laughed mirthlessly and then explained that they had been given to Elise and Frances by the fairies. They were fairy rings made from fairy silver.

"The Yorkshireman went on to tell me that they are a pair, and can never be separated. If the two rings are ever taken to different locations, separate rooms, different tabletops, they would always find their way, uncannily, back to each other.

"While the man was talking, I suddenly noticed that the rings were in my hand. I hadn't noticed the man give them to me, yet there they were – in my grip. They felt warm and seemed to vibrate gently.

"'Fairy silver?' I asked, trying to smile. 'But you don't believe in fairies, do you?'

"The man looked me dead in the eye and said, 'Of course I believe in fairies you bloody idiot! They live at the bottom of my bloody garden! What makes you think I don't believe in the accursed creatures?! Did I ever say that?!' And with that, the man physically picked me up by the scruff of the neck and threw me out of the front door.

"I realised that there was no point protesting or banging on the door to regain admittance. I had most decidedly outstayed my welcome. The rain was still lashing down and my overcoat was still drying in the house's kitchen. However, I thought better of trying to retrieve it, and began the long trudge towards Bradford and the train station with my hands shoved deep into my trouser pockets.

"It was only after walking for some 30 minutes that I realised that I still had the two so-called fairy rings in my clenched fist," I held up the two silver rings. "*These* two fairy rings."

Campbell and Jones were silent for a moment, and then it was Campbell who spoke up. "So what do they do, old man?" he inquired. "These so-called fairy rings?"

And so I showed him.

I asked Jones to clasp his hands together as though he were making a desperate prayer, and hold the clasped hands out before him. Then I asked him to extend his two forefingers as though they were two separate church steeples reaching up to the sky.

"You will remember," I said, "the words of Arthur Wright when he said that the two rings can never be apart, that they will always find their way back to each other? Well watch this..."

I placed a fairy ring onto each of Jones' extended forefingers. The rings were too small to go over his knuckles, or even very far down the first phalange, so I merely allowed them to rest were they stopped.

"Concentrate on the gap between the forefingers and the rings," I instructed, "and just allow this to happen."

Slowly, inexorably, the fingers moved together until the rings touched each other.

"You see?" I asked.

Jones took the rings from his fingers and examined them in silence.

"I can see you need more evidence," I said, and we conducted a second experiment.

I took the two rings from Jones and instructed him to stand with his arms and hands outstretched before him. His arms were straight, and were held out at right angles from his body.

Once again I pushed the rings onto an outstretched finger, one ring per hand. "Now focus on the gap between your hands," I instructed him. "Focus on the gap, and feel the rings pulling together, almost as though they were both huge magnets, attracted by each other and forced to pull towards each other."

Nothing happened for a moment and I feared that the fairy magic had deserted me. But then slowly Jones' hands began to be drawn towards each other, and within a few moments the rings were once more touching each other.

"A fascinating display, is it not?" I enquired.

"Indeed," said Campbell. "And these rings, they were in the position of the Wright family in Cottingley, you say?"

"Absolutely," I confirmed.

"What say you, Jones?" asked Campbell.

"Fascinating," was all Jones could say as he gazed at the rings in awe.

The grandfather clock in the hallway chimed midnight. The old year was finished, the new year had begun.

"Happy 1923, gentlemen!" I smiled.

"Best wishes for the new year, old man!" laughed Campbell, and he shook my hand heartily.

"Fascinating," said Jones, still observing the rings.

"I fear that he's in a world of his own," sighed Campbell. "Too much brandy would be my diagnosis! Don't worry old man, I'll see him safely to his door."

And with that the two men, aided by George the butler, donned their overcoats, put hats upon heads. and set out into the chill, fresh January night air.

I wonder how long it was before Jones realised that he was still carrying the silver fairy rings? Considering the amount of brandy that he'd put away, not until the next morning, I'll wager. Not that I care of course, I was just pleased to be rid of the damned things. They're his problem to worry about now, thank the good Lord.

The fairy rings are, of course, cursed. Over the past year my business had been failing, my wife had left me in the most scandalous of circumstances which involved the coachman, the contents of my strongbox, and a new life in South Africa, and I had been forced to dismiss all of my staff save for the ever-loyal George.

Yes, the rings were cursed; Elsie and Francis' father had been quite right about that. Cursed and damned, and just as the canny Yorkshireman tricked me into taking the rings away from their little, terraced house that stormy afternoon in Cottingley, so I had pulled the same act of legerdemain to dump the unholy things on to Jones.

*

Our Host's Secret

Ah, there you are, dear reader! I thought for one moment that I had lost you, scared off perhaps by all my talk of curses and errant wives! But no, here you are, and most welcome you are too.

We have already spoken earlier, during the episode of the clockmaker's pendulum, about the effect of so-called ideomotor phenomenon. This is the action by which a pendulum can be made to move without the volunteer feeling that they are doing anything to encourage it, and likewise it is attributed to what makes the pointing device move atop an Ouija board. A very similar phenomenon is at work here, both with the fingers and the hands being drawn together.

The finger routine is actually a physical trick whereby with the hands and majority of fingers clenched together, the two outstretched fingers cannot help but be drawn together. I would encourage you to try it for yourself. Clench your hands together as though deep in prayer, then allow your forefingers on both hands to stretch upwards like twin church spires. The fingers will be between half an inch and an inch apart. Hold your hands before your face, focus on the gap between the forefingers, and watch in awe as they are drawn irresistibly together. Normally within a few seconds the fingers will touch.

Likewise, with the hands. With the arms outstretched, the weight of the arms means that they will begin to be drawn together in a matter of seconds.

The finger routine will work for practically everyone, whereas some people can resist the arm routine if they really want to. However, in my experience most people will fall for it within 30 seconds – some (most) much faster than that. The important aspect is to encourage the volunteer to concentrate on the gap (whether between the fingers or the hands) and 'just let it happen'.

As with the pendulum demonstration, choosing the right victim, er, I mean *volunteer,* will help immensely, as will the creation of a conducive atmosphere, but try not to lose too much sleep over those aspects. These demonstrations work perfectly well for the vast majority of people. Hypnotists and magicians have been using them for decades and centuries to very good effect. There is no reason why you cannot do likewise.

The rings are of course superfluous. They are not required for the phenomena to take place. However, in this routine they are used as the actual *explanation* for the phenomena – they are the catalyst.

Having these physical objects as the reason for the phenomena encourages an even higher percentage of success in my experience. I believe this is because responsibility is taken off the shoulders of the volunteer. It is not the volunteer's fault that the phenomena are occurring, it is the fault of the rings. Therefore, the volunteer becomes more relaxed and is not afraid to just 'go with it'. The volunteer has nothing to prove nor disprove.

Any rings can be used for this routine. The description of my dinner party demonstration talks about small silver rings, and they are simply perfect if you can find them (try the same *New Age* and *hippy* shops as for the pendulums, both brick & mortar and on-line, and also try toe rings or children's rings to get the right size), however it is as easy to mention 'fairy gold' as 'fairy silver', and don't worry if the rings you want to use are adult size, it's not a problem.

I never try to force the rings over the volunteer's knuckles. Just let them drop onto the first phalange of the finger and allow them to rest where they stop. This action is also good at encouraging the belief amongst your guests that the rings are smaller than they actually are, if you're using adult size rings. We *are* terrible cheats, are we not?

*

Sherlock Holmes Says...

The *Cottingley Fairies* incident refers to a series of five photographs taken by Elsie Wright and Frances Griffiths, two young cousins who lived together in small house with Elsie's mother and father on Main Street in the village of Cottingley, near Bradford, England.

In 1917, when the first two photographs were taken, Elsie was sixteen years old and Frances was nine.

The pictures came to the attention of my dear creator, Sir Arthur Conan Doyle. As fate would have it, he had been commissioned by the Strand magazine to write an article on fairies for the Christmas 1920 edition of the magazine. Arthur Conan Doyle decided to use the photographs to illustrate this article. Doyle was a confirmed Spiritualist, and was a fervent supporter of the photographs, claiming them to be genuine, and conclusive proof of the existence of the esoteric and supernatural.

Public reaction at the time was somewhat mixed with some accepting the images as genuine while others believed them to be fakes. As the years have progressed and the general public has become more sophisticated in the use of technology, this level of disbelief increased, and in the 21st Century it would be difficult to imagine anyone who would look at these photographs and declare them to be anything but crude fakes.

Many have wondered, myself included, as to how a man who created the world's greatest detective (I say this with no false modesty), a man lauded for his analytical and logical mind, could not only believe in the existence of fairies, but also be a fervent supporter of Spiritualism, even when all the evidence pointed to the whole sorry affair being populated by charlatans and cheats.

"I pondered this conundrum for quite some time, it was indeed a *two pipe problem*, until I came to the realisation that human beings are not simple two-dimensional creatures. They are very much made up in all three dimensions. They can in one moment be kind and caring, and in the next cruel and mean. Their beliefs change with the wind, they are contradictory creatures, whose opinions and ideas are fickle and are often based merely on their so-called *gut instinct*, with little or no regard for rhyme and reason.

Arthur Conan Doyle, in his creation of an analytical Great Detective whilst also believing in fairies and ghosts and spirits, was displaying no-more contradiction than practically the whole of humanity.

In his support of the Cottingley girls and Spiritualism, Arthur Conan Doyle merely demonstrates to us that he was human. A man often-times driven by emotion rather than logic, and in that he differs not one jot with the rest of humanity (myself, of course, excepted).

Like Freud with his cocaine, Arthur Conan Doyle's belief system was nothing more than a crutch with which he could support himself. And perhaps this was never so true as after the death of his beloved son, Arthur Alleyne 'Kingsley', during World War One. Aged just twenty-four, Arthur Conan Doyle's son died tragically close to the end of hostilities.

It was a loss that many observers said Arthur Conan Doyle never truly recovered from, and if this led the man to find some small solace in his belief in the fairies of Cottingley, then so be it, say I.

*

Nous Continuons...

With Jones, Campbell, and those damned fairy rings safely parcelled off into the night, and the hour growing increasingly late, I was minded to retire to my chamber for the evening.

I made my way towards the kitchen with the intention of dismissing George for the evening. I must admit to being a little unsteady on my feet. The New Year's Eve meal and accompanying beverages had, I concede, left me a little light headed.

I was just about to reach for the kitchen door, when the door opened by itself and through it emerged George, the very man himself.

"Ah, sir!" he exclaimed. "I was just about to come looking for you. You have a visitor, sir. Wiggins."

"Wiggins?" I echoed. "What the deuce does Wiggins want at this hour?"

"It appears he has a little *something* for you sir. An item of interest."

"Ah, very well," I sighed, pulling wide the kitchen door and entering. "Let us see what Wiggins is looking to sell to me now."

In all fairness, Wiggins was a good man. Oh yes, he was a thief, a pick-pocket, a cheat and a liar, but those few faults aside, he was my best contact when it came to obtaining Holmes and Doyle related paraphernalia. All of the items he managed to obtain were strictly *black market*, but this did not phase me. After all, a collector must collect.

THE COLLECTOR COLLECTS

I found Wiggins perched on a stool next to the stove, holding gloved hands out towards the heat. On noticing me enter, he stood up, doffed his bowler hat, and allowed a semblance of a smile to break across his stubble tarnished face.

"Sir," he said.

"Wiggins," I replied, taking a packet of cigarettes from my jacket pocket and lighting one. "Exceedingly late to be making house calls, do you not think?"

The man ignored my question. "He's back," he said simply, triumphantly, his Cockney accent permeating the air.

"Who?" I enquired.

"Him! Arthur Conan Doyle!"

"Well of course he's back," I replied. "He's been back from the United States for almost six months now."

Doyle had spent the first half of 1922 in the Unites States of America, lecturing predominantly on the subject of Spiritualism.

"No!" said Wiggins. "I mean he's *back*. Back doing séances with his missus!"

"Really?" Wiggins' presence had suddenly become a lot more interesting. "Carry on."

The news that Jean Leckie, the wife of Doyle, was once more hosting séances in London was of no small interest to me. Leckie fancied herself a spirit-medium, a belief that Doyle was only too keen to encourage. Hopefully Wiggins had some interesting titbits of information about their exploits.

"Well, I was at a bit of a loose end this evening, not being one that gets invited to social gatherings all that often, so I thinks to myself, 'Wiggins, old boy, whatcha going to do tonight?' Then the thought struck me. It's New Year's Eve! There's a good bet that old Sir Arthur Conan Doyle will be heading out to celebrate in his own inimitable style. Why don't I just tag along, follow him as it were, and see what he gets up to? Just in case there was anything of interest that I could report back to you."

"Yes, yes," I said impatiently. "Do try and get on with it, Wiggins." Wiggins was, as you are probably becoming aware, a weaver of tales, and could take minutes before reaching the point of any given story.

"Well," he continued, "as the evening wore on, it became apparent that him and his wife weren't going to be headed out. Rather, they had guests coming round to *them.* Must have been a half-dozen carriages rolled up, one after the other, with the great and the good being deposited and shown through into the Doyle's home.

"Once I figured that all the guests had arrived, curiosity got the better of me, so I hopped over the garden fence and creeped up to the parlour window. From my vantage point I could make them all out, chatting amicably, and being served a sherry or something not unlike. But it didn't take them long to settle down to the real business of the evening. They all sat around the big dining table, held hands with each other, and started in with the séance.

"I was a bit wary of being collared, sitting there in the garden with my nose pushed up against the window, so once I knew what they were up to, I made my way back out on to the street, and observed from a distance.

"Must have been two hours later when they all began to re-emerge from the house. All the cabs started to queue up, and old Doyle himself came out of the house and onto the street to orchestrate proceedings, making sure that all of his guests got into the right cab. And right then, that's when I made my move!"

Wiggins looked at me triumphantly. I had no idea what he was referring to, but clearly he was waiting for me to be impressed.

"Your move?" I asked. "Pray continue."

"I stumbles across the road like I'm some old lush," he said, "and I bumps right in to Doyle. Nearly knocked the old boy flying, I did! 'I say!' he bellows, chest all puffed out. 'Watch where you're going, my man!' I mumbles an apology, still pretending to be drunk, see? Then I staggers away up the road."

I was somewhat underwhelmed. "And...?"

"And this, sir!" exclaimed Wiggins, and he pulled a small pamphlet out from his inside jacket pocket. "I purloined it right out of Doyle's own pocket when I bumped into him. Took it right out his pocket, so I did, and he never noticed a bloomin' thing!"

"What is it?" I enquired, taking the pamphlet from Wiggins' hands.

I regarded the pamphlet's cover. In an ornate font it read:

The Spirit-Medium's

Secret Friend

And below the title, in a stern, bold font, were the words...

FOR PRIVATE CONSUMPTION ONLY!

NOT FOR THE EYES OF THE GENERAL PUBLIC OR LAITY!

Opening up the pamphlet, I quickly skimmed over the first page which was entirely devoted to an advertisement:

Are you a spirit-medium looking for your proper home? Mr. Baginski's bed & breakfast at no.24 Flower & Dean Street, Spitalfields, London offers rooms at very competitive rates, aimed exclusively at those of a spiritual nature. Don't delay – pop round today!

The next page, under the heading 'Introduction':

We are all spirit. Despite the fact that we occupy mortal bodies in this mortal sphere, the truth remains that we come from spirit, spirit resides within us, and that we will once more return to spirit when our days upon this earth have ended.

And so-on and so-forth in a similar vein. This was, so far, pretty standard Spiritualist stuff. Although I was interested in the pamphlet due to the fact that it had belonged to Doyle, the contents were hardly ground-breaking.

I flicked through several pages, and my eyes came to rest of another paragraph, under the heading 'Developing Spirit-Mediumship':

The spirits hear and understand our every thought. When those thoughts are good and pure and earnest, the spirits may respond. Perhaps they endeavour to answer questions, to guide our way, or present to us truths, if only we had the ears and the wherewithal to hear. A belief in spirit-mediumship of course carries with it the assumption that spirits are trying to communicate with us, and that we may develop our senses to hear the words that are being whispered to us from the spirit realm.

And several pages on...

Studying and learning spirit-mediumship in a home circle is perhaps the most preferable way. In a home circle, like-minded friends can gather to attempt spirit communication in an atmosphere of mutual trust and understanding. Public circles may be attended, but often a level of suspicion may arise at such meetings where a spirit-medium is being paid to lead the circle. Suspicion and mistrust have a negative effect on a sensitive medium and good results can often be hard to find at such open public meetings.

And...

The thought that there may be evil or dangerous spirits in the séance room is a bad one. To believe in the possibility of unsavoury spirits interacting within the circle is damaging to the possibility of good results. If a circle has only good thoughts, and the spirit-medium leading the circle is possessed only of harmonious and positive intent, then evil spirits will not be drawn into the circle. Only a circle with evil intent or populated by those who are inspired by greed and avarice will attract spirits of a similar disposition.

"Somewhat interesting," I said, looking up at Wiggins. "But only because this is Conan Doyle's copy. The contents are rather run-of-the-mill, I'm afraid. The usual kind of Spiritualist nonsense."

"No, no!" said Wiggins, coming over to me as I leant against the kitchen wall. "If I may, sir, you're missing the point entirely."

He took the pamphlet from me, and flicked through, looking for a specific page. At last he found it, and thrust the pamphlet back to me, pointing at a particular passage.

I read, under the heading 'The Spirit is Weak'...

Spirit-mediums should not be obliged to sit in circle or conduct séances when they are not well, or when not in the proper mood. In certain circumstances, perhaps when the rent is due, or the children need clothes, or the grocer's bill must be paid, the poor soul, through actual need, may be required to misuse his or her sacred gifts in the earnest desire to satisfy the sitter and earn the money necessary to keep his or her little family together.

In these circumstances, these little tips may lighten the load of the sensitive spirit-medium and allow them to traverse the path of light a little easier.

1. *A veritable encyclopedia of knowledge may be gathered from servants simply by asking of them the simplest of questions. When arriving at a lady's home in order to sit in séance, a harmless statement such as, "I am sensing a lot of sadness in this house," aimed at the lady's maid will often illicit a veritable waterfall of information from said maid. The lower classes are known for their enjoyment of gossip, and with a little encouragement and a kindly smile, much information can be received that can then be repeated as being from spirit while in the séance room.*

2. *The daily newspapers can be a mine of information. A spirit-medium would be wise to keep up to date with the latest news, particularly from the society*

pages, in order to not miss out on any interesting tit-bits ascertaining to his or her clients.

3. *In a completely dark séance room, it is possible for the spirit-medium to have his or her neighbour believing themselves to be holding either the right or left hand of the medium while in fact the neighbours are actually both holding the same hand. This of course leaves the spirit medium with a free hand with which to aid and encourage the spirits to communicate with the sitters, perhaps via the touching of the those sat close by or by rapping upon the table. The spirit-medium should, of course, ensure that total blackout is achieved before attempting such an aid.*

4. *Flowers delivered by spirit are known to live for a long time, sometimes as long as a year. When earth bound flowers in vases have withered and died, flowers brought from spirit will continue to adorn any room for months after they were first placed in water. This can be achieved by adding a little glycerin to the water in the flower's vase.*

5. *To make any object luminous, the spirit-medium should purchase a tin of luminous paint. This paint should then be thinned with turpentine and strips of cloth soaked in it. Once the strips of cloth have been allowed to dry for several days, when they are vigorously shaken a fine, luminous powder will fall.*

This powder can then be collected and used to cover any object.

6. *The power of the spirits may be demonstrated by the spirit-medium having himself or herself blind-folded. With a blind-fold tied around his or her eyes, the spirit-medium may still be able to discern colours or words in a book or point to and name people in the room. It is a little known fact that even the most tightly knotted blind-fold will still afford the wearer a modicum of sight, particularly if the subject frowns and closes his/her eyes as the blind-fold is administered and then allows his or her eyes to open and raises the eyebrows once the blind-fold is in place.*

7. *A like-minded friend or colleague may be utilised in a séance room employing absolute darkness. The friend can walk around the circle, tapping sitters on the shoulder, whispering in their ears, or blowing on their cheeks, thereby relieving the pressure on the spirits to manifest such phenomena themselves.*

8. *In such a darkened environment as the séance room, a small amount of thread may be secretly used to encourage items such as tambourines or candles to move of the spirit's volition.*

9. *By insisting on absolute darkness in the séance room, the spirit-medium's ability to aid the spirits in their task is limited only by the imagination. The techniques employed need not be overly-elaborate*

and contrived. Something as simple to achieve as a booted foot kicking at the underside of the séance table will prove equally as effective as any complicated piece of apparatus. However, discretion is recommended in all cases, and of course it is far more preferable for the spirits themselves to manifest and create genuine phenomena.

I read in silence for five minutes, maybe more. After digesting the final point, I placed the pamphlet down on the kitchen table and smiled across and Wiggins, who returned the smile.

"Do you not see it now, sir?" he said, gleefully. "He knows! He knows it's all falsehood and chicanery, and yet he continues to hold séances and lecture on the genuine nature of Spiritualism! And his wife, I can't imagine that she hasn't read the same booklet also, sir! The pair of them, in cahoots!"

"He knows," I reaffirmed, almost in a whisper. "The old dog knows it's all fake. How much, Wiggins? For the pamphlet, how much?"

"A £1 note, sir?" said Wiggins. It was more of an opening gambit than a statement, but I was too tired, too drunk, too *elated* to argue.

"A £1 note, it is!" I smiled and handed over the money.

With that, Wiggins took his leave, wishing me a very happy new year and shaking my hand most vigorously, as though we were partners on some manner of quest and had just made an important discovery or break-through. In a way, I suppose, that was at least partway true.

EPILOGUE – THE CAT GETS HIS CREAM

With Wiggins paid and cheerfully departed into the chill night air, George locked and bolted the kitchen door. This task complete, I dismissed him for the evening and retired to my study. Rather than head straight to bed, which had been my first plan, I decided to peruse Doyle's *Spirit-Medium's Secret Friend* a little more with yet another glass of brandy. It was, after all, New Year's Eve and I probably would not rise much before noon the following day.

I was disturbed some 10 minutes later by a gentle tapping upon the front door. With George dismissed for the evening, I was forced to answer the door myself. Who should be standing there upon my doorstep but the delightful Miss Carriger, *sans mama*!

"Miss Carriger?" I enquired, attempting to disguise the brandy induced slur in my voice. "How delightful, won't you come in? All is well, I trust?"

"Oh, my good sir, everything is wonderful!" beamed Miss Carriger. "I simply could not sleep after witnessing the marvellous demonstrations of your artefacts. I had to return, to thank you in person. I left mother asleep, snoring if the truth be known, in front of our log fire, and slipped out of the back door like a common thief," she giggled excitedly at the thought. "The servants were all in their quarters, so nobody knows that I am here!"

I took Miss Carriger's coat and invited her into my study. Her hair was tousled, no longer piled high upon her head, and there was a look of wild liberation in her eyes.

"A brandy?" I asked her. "Or perhaps a small glass of wine?"

Suddenly Miss Carriger was by my side and her arm was around my shoulder in a very forward manner, most unbecoming of a lady of her standing.

"How about a *large* glass of wine," she whispered in a demeanour that her mother would surely disapprove of, "and a kiss?"

With those accursed fairy rings no longer in my possession, it seemed as though my luck had changed at last. First I discover that old man Doyle is at the very least aware of his beloved Spiritualism's fraudulence, and then the divine Miss Carriger makes an unaccompanied night visit! 1923 was, it seemed, going to be a very good year.

"You see," continued Miss Carriger, whispering into my ear, "I do so enjoy your company, Mr. Moriarty. I find you most... *intoxicating!*"

"Oh, please," I replied with a sly grin, "call me James."

FIN

Also from MX Publishing

MX Publishing is the world's largest specialist Sherlock Holmes publisher, with over a hundred titles and fifty authors creating the latest in Sherlock Holmes fiction and non-fiction.

From traditional short stories and novels to travel guides and quiz books, MX Publishing cater for all Holmes fans.

The collection includes leading titles such as *Benedict Cumberbatch In Transition* and *The Norwood Author* which won the 2011 Howlett Award (Sherlock Holmes Book of the Year).

MX Publishing also has one of the largest communities of Holmes fans on Facebook with regular contributions from dozens of authors.

www.mxpublishing.com

Also from MX Publishing

The Missing Authors Series

Sherlock Holmes and The Adventure of The Grinning Cat
Sherlock Holmes and The Nautilus Adventure
Sherlock Holmes and The Round Table Adventure

"Joseph Svec, III is brilliant in entwining two endearing and enduring classics of literature, blending the factual with the fantastical; the playful with the pensive; and the mischievous with the mysterious. We shall, all of us young and old, benefit with a cup of tea, a tranquil afternoon, and a copy of Sherlock Holmes, The Adventure of the Grinning Cat."
Amador County Holmes Hounds Sherlockian Society

www.mxpublishing.com

Also from MX Publishing

Our bestselling books are our short story collections;

'Lost Stories of Sherlock Holmes' , 'The Outstanding Mysteries of Sherlock Holmes', The Papers of Sherlock Holmes Volume 1 and 2, 'Untold Adventures of Sherlock Holmes' (and the sequel 'Studies in Legacy) and 'Sherlock Holmes in Pursuit', 'The Cotswold Werewolf and Other Stories of Sherlock Holmes' – and many more……

www.mxpublishing.com

Also from MX Publishing

The American Literati Series

The Final Page of Baker Street
The Baron of Brede Place
Seventeen Minutes To Baker Street

"The really amazing thing about this book is the author's ability to call up the 'essence' of both the Baker Street 'digs' of Holmes and Watson as well as that of the 'mean streets' of Marlowe's Los Angeles. Although none of the action takes place in either place, Holmes and Watson share a sense of camaraderie and self-confidence in facing threats and problems that also pervades many of the later tales in the Canon. Following their conversations and banter is a return to Edwardian England and its certainties and hope for the future. This is definitely the world before The Great War."
Philip K Jones

www.mxpublishing.com

Also from MX Publishing

The Detective and The Woman Series

The Detective and The Woman
The Detective, The Woman and The Winking Tree
The Detective, The Woman and The Silent Hive

"The book is entertaining, puzzling and a lot of fun. I believe the author has hit on the only type of long-term relationship possible for Sherlock Holmes and Irene Adler. The details of the narrative only add force to the romantic defects we expect in both of them and their growth and development are truly marvelous to watch. This is not a love story. Instead, it is a coming-of-age tale starring two of our favorite characters."
Philip K Jones

www.mxpublishing.com

Also from MX Publishing

The Sherlock Holmes and Enoch Hale Series

The Amateur Executioner
The Poisoned Penman
The Egyptian Curse

"The Amateur Executioner: Enoch Hale Meets Sherlock Holmes", the first collaboration between Dan Andriacco and Kieran McMullen, concerns the possibility of a Fenian attack in London. Hale, a native Bostonian, is a reporter for London's Central News Syndicate - where, in 1920, Horace Harker is still a familiar figure, though far from revered. "The Amateur Executioner" takes us into an ambiguous and murky world where right and wrong aren't always distinguishable. I look forward to reading more about Enoch Hale."
Sherlock Holmes Society of London

www.mxpublishing.com

www.ingramcontent.com/pod-product-compliance
Lightning Source LLC
Chambersburg PA
CBHW071311130626
46556CB00004B/1559